Shores

of

Tripoli

FOR LITERARY HEAT

www.BarbarianSpy.com

This book is copyright © Dirk Hessian
Published by BarbarianSpy in 2016
Cover design © S Bush 2016
Cover image: © Kornilovdream | Dreamstime.com
ISBN Print 978-1-925190-70-0
All rights reserved

"Shores of Tripoli is a work of historical fiction. Apart from the well-known actual people, events, and locales that figure in the narrative, all names, characters, places, and incidents are the products of the author's imagination or are used fictitiously. Any resemblance to current events or locales, or to living persons, is entirely coincidental.

Shores of Tripoli

by

Dirk Hessian

~

CONTENTS

Chapter One:

Boston, 1802

Billy Evans stood at the window overlooking Foster Lane when Henry Gawn called out to him from the bed.

"Come back to me, boy. Standing in the window in that state will draw unwanted attention."

"I think there is not time for more, Mr. Gawn. The dawn is upon us and Mistress Marianne said she would be home from her sister's early today."

It was not that the young apprentice would not willingly return to his master's arms. Henry, the printer of the *Boston Sentinel* broadsheet, who Billy's father, William senior, a textile manufacturer, had indentured him to in the failed hope to reign in his proclivities, cocked quite well. In his endeavor to "save" his son, William senior had tragically erred, although he did not realize it—nor would it be the last time he did so. Rather than the young men of Billy's age who he had been observed cavorting with, his father had unwittingly turned him over to a more seasoned and experienced man of the same nature, which was more to Billy's taste.

Resisting the call of the cock was more a matter of lack of time—the chores that Billy had to accomplish this day before he was free for the next two. His eyes were cast beyond the end of Foster Lane, where it spilled into Ship Street and, beyond that, the ships' masts at Clarke's Shipyard and Hutchinson's wharf. The first golden rays of Friday were glinting through the ship's masts there, making Billy pine for the sea and for the danger the one he marked as his true lover represented.

He heard the whistle and looked down into the street, where his sometimes friend, Ned, the solitary figure out and about at this time, was standing on the cobblestones and looking up at Billy's naked body leaning on the frame of Henry Gawn's bedroom window. Ned was grinning. He thrust his pelvis forward and made a rude gesture of masturbating with one hand, while giving a fingers'-circle signal with the other that the plans were in place. In exchange for a fuck, Ned, who had brought produce to market from his family's farm south of the city, had agreed to drop Billy off in the small harbor village of Shernhaven as he was returning home.

Billy gave a small wave and turned away from the window. It had been in search of this assurance that had drawn him from Henry's bed to the vantage point. The mere thought of the assignation in Shernhaven and the two days of relief from the demanding work of printer's apprentice because of the coming high holiday made him harden, a response that did not go unnoticed by Henry.

"Ah to be so young and to rise so quickly," Henry murmured. "Marianne will dawdle. I know she will. There is plenty of time for another fucking. It will be days before I can have you again. Come to me."

Laughing, quietly, Billy moved to the bed. "You are not so old that you cannot harden thrice in a night."

"Aye, and twice in a morning when I have as nice a piece as you. I wish that I can keep the image of you naked in the sunlight at the window until I can be inside you again. You are so young and perfectly formed. I want to imprison you to my will, nail you to the wall with my cock. Here, do not make me wait. I ache for you."

Billy shivered at the image of being dominated so. When he reached the side of the bed, the older man—yet barely thirty to Billy's eighteen—grabbed Billy's trim waist in his beefy hands and easily lifted the smaller, curly headed, raven-haired, handsome youth and settled Billy's knees on either side of his gray-laced strawberry-blond hairy and burly chest. Billy leaned forward, gripping the top of the headboard in his fists and laying his cheek against the flower-wallpapered wall. Henry opened his mouth over Billy's cock and both sighed as Billy started to slowly move his hips. After several minutes, Billy came upright, moved his hands behind him to find Henry's plump, hard cock, and positioned its bulb inside his channel opening. Then, as he sank down on Henry's cock with a groan and a moan, he leaned back to lay his torso flat on the surface of the bed and let his arms go slack at his sides, after which the older man pulled leather straps tight around Billy's thighs and calves to tighten the younger man's channel on his buried cock. Then, supporting Billy's bound legs against his chest, a grunting Henry used the strength of his hand holds on the young man's waist to pull and push the belabored channel on the cock.

Billy groaned at the tightness of the fuck in a channel collapsed by the binding of his legs. "Yes, yes, punish me."

Later, with Billy cupped into Henry's belly, it was evident that the printer wanted his apprentice again.

"It's late, and I have so much to do today before I can leave. You promised me . . . oh, no! Oh, god!"

It was too late. Henry had already entered him in a sidesplit and was pinching Billy's nipples hard between thumbs and forefingers, giving Billy the roughness that aroused him the most.

"Just this once more. You may trim your work to meet your time needs. I cannot resist—"

"We shall see little one. Remember that it is you who are indentured to me. Whenever I want to take you, I will."

Billy sighed at the forcefulness of the statement, which matched the strong thrusts of the man's cock.

They both heard the electrifying click of the street door two stories down at the same moment. Someone—doubtless Mistress Marianne—was in the shop and would be mounting the stairs to the upper floors, where the printer and his apprentice lived, at any moment.

Four bare feet hit the floor as quickly and silently as possible, and Billy gathered his clothes and headed for his space in the attic while Henry pulled his own clothing on and stuffed the leather strappings he had been using with Billy in the bottom drawer of a bureau. Henry would detain his wife on some excuse of why he was not yet in his shop while Billy stole by them and went into the rear yard and began chores that would fool Mistress Marianne that he was already up and about.

The two had this down to a routine. They had lingered before and, if Henry had any power over the matter, they would linger again and again for the two years remaining on Billy's indenture. Never had Henry had such a sweet ass and beautiful young man under his control. A lad who sought out the punishment that aroused the printer in the giving. And not the least amusement was that Billy's pompous ass of a father had sent the young man to him for protection, begging him not to tell the reason why he was indenturing him rather than sending him to college, where he would be only loosely supervised and other attractive young men would be present in abundance. The father thought the threat was from other young men. Henry had every reason to know, however, that young Billy preferred the experience of older men—men of power and danger and who would punish Billy a bit, as pleased him. The printer knew that Billy actually welcomed the danger of being discovered by Mistress Marianne.

And, another amusement, Henry thus would not tell Billy that Marianne knew of Henry's proclivities and did not care in the least as long as Henry kept a roof over her head and fine food on the table—and did not trouble her with conjugal demands. The only real danger was that the buxom Marianne fancied the young man herself.

* * * *

"I think this would be a good place to pull off."

"Aye, I agree it would," Billy answered Ned. It was on the wrong side of Shernhaven—on the headland overlooking the town from the north and the sea. Billy's assignation was in a cove below the cliffs to the south of the town. But Billy didn't want Ned to know where or who he was meeting. The twilight of the Friday Billy last lay with the printer was lingering, and it soon would be dark. But there was plenty of time.

Ned pulled the wagon off the track and through a copse of trees and almost to the edge of the cliff overlooking the sea to the east. They could see down into the bowl at the harbor's edge where Shernhaven was located, but there were a few large house's of the town's wealthy on the headlands between where the wagon was brought to a halt and the town. Flickering lamplight was beginning to illuminate the windows of two of these houses. But the young men were quite sure they couldn't be seen from there, because they were clothed in greater darkness and curtained off by the thin, wavering trunks of birch trees whispering in the breeze coming off the water.

Ned set the brake of the wagon with one hand while he was moving the other arm around Billy's shoulders. Billy leaned in toward him, knowing this was the time for payment for the wagon ride and Ned's silence and goodwill. They kissed.

Billy was glad of the darkness as Ned was ugly—tall and gangly—and although he talked a ruffian's talk, he had proven to be awkward and unimaginative in the fuck. He was two years older than Billy. He had been respected among some at school, however, because he possessed a long cock and used it liberally. Just a few months earlier, as the end of the last school term had passed, he had taken Billy by force, with two others holding Billy down. But what Ned hadn't known, was that the schoolmaster had been at Billy before he had and a rough man on the road once before that. Billy had had to be forced by Ned because Ned was ugly and a bully, and Billy didn't know until he was being fucked how deep Ned could cock. Once the cock was inside him and Ned had punched him in the mouth to subdue him, Billy didn't care how ugly or bullying Ned was. Ned had thought that he had charmed Billy with his cock when Billy cried out for it half way through the fuck and gave Ned a ride he'd never forget. He didn't know that it was the very forced nature of the act— the closed fist to the cheek—that had turned Billy on. Now that Billy knew—and knowing that it was too dark to have any concern for Ned's ugliness, Billy didn't mind the fare he had to pay. It would be a straightforward poke this time, but the scene in which it was set was a sign that Ned had control over him. That was what Billy needed.

* * * *

11

The schoolmaster, Samuel Hale, was barely five years older than Billy. He was handsome, with red hair and a broad chest and arm muscles that belied his profession as a teacher. He lived in a small cottage beside the schoolhouse, and Billy found himself gravitating to the man. Coming to the schoolhouse even when school was not in session. Asking for extra instruction. Sometimes he'd come when Sam was doing his chores. One afternoon Billy arrived when Sam was chopping wood, stripped to the waist. His torso was magnificent, but Billy saw marks of the whip on him. Asking, Sam merely said that he'd had a rough childhood. Billy had recently become familiar with rough, and the mere mention of the word aroused him, although he didn't understand why. Maybe this man gave it as rough as he'd received it, Billy thought.

Billy had had a rough initiation too.

He had skipped school one fine afternoon a few weeks previous to his encounter with the schoolmaster and had been walking aimlessly along the road south toward Shernhaven, not having any goal or plan, but knowing only that it was too nice of a day to be in school. As he walked, a wagon pulled up beside him. A burley Irishman with flaming red hair hailed him.

"Would this be the road to Boston?"

"Yes, you're on the right road, mister."

"And I guess you would be knowing why young men like yourself dally around on this section to the track, would you not?"

No Billy didn't know. But he found the question so strange that he passed over it and didn't answer.

"You're a right handsome young man. Not too old for schooling, though, I don't imagine. You look more than a bit too young to be standing in this stretch. Maybe it's the smallness."

"Old enough," Billy responded indignantly, pulling himself up to stand straighter. His lack of height was one of the biggest of life's irritations for him. He was always being taken for a few years younger than his near nineteen years.

"So, where you off to?"

"Nowhere in particular."

"No one down the road expecting you or anything?"

"No, just out for the exercise."

The man gave a guttural laugh at that response, which he took for saucy teasing. "I could give a strapping young man like you all the exercise he could want. I got to admit I'm really right randy now, and you have that look about you that makes a man go hard and that wants to be poked. Fancy a fuck? I've got chickens in the back. Fair exchange it would be."

"What?" Billy managed in a strangled voice, confused and scared but also inexplicably aroused. The man had set the brake on the wagon and was coming down off it. He was huge, maybe twice Billy's weight. Billy felt frightened, but all a tingle at the same time. He turned and ran into the woods at the side of the road.

That was a mistake. "Ah, a playful one we have here. You best not make me work too hard for it," the man called out at Billy's retreating back. "You would regret that soundly, I can tell you."

The man caught Billy easily and dragged him farther into the trees to a small glade where a few large trees had been chopped down, leaving stumps at near chair height.

The man grabbed Billy's arm and spun him around. "No!" Billy cried out. But then all of the air was knocked out of him as the man punched him in the stomach with a doubled-up fist and, as Billy bent over from that blow, gave him an upper cut to the jaw for good measure.

The ruffian was already fumbling at Billy's clothes as Billy was sinking to the ground. He had Billy's shirt opened down the front and the front of his trousers opened and hanging low on his hips.

"No!" Billy managed to stumble out in slurred words, but the man pulled him up by his shirt collar and backhanded his face twice. Billy hit the ground hard, and the man stooped down, grabbed the waistband of Billy's trousers, and pulled them and his underdrawers off his legs. His hands then immediately went to unbuttoning his own fly.

The man laughed, looking down at Billy. "Well, look there. You already want me."

Billy was embarrassed as well as dazed. He indeed felt that he'd gone half hard. He looked up at the man's crotch, at the already erect cock the man was holding in his hand. More

13

mesmerizing to Billy was the bush of red, kinky hair that surrounded the root of it. Billy moaned and tried to move away. A heavy boot plopped down in the center of his chest.

"You ain't gonna give me trouble now, are you? You want the fuck. We both know that."

Pinned to the ground, Billy just whimpered incoherently. He couldn't hide that he was going hard, though. Being assaulted and controlled like this—not being able to do anything about it—had aroused him in ways he'd never achieved by himself in bed at night. The danger of it. It was exhilarating.

The ruffian hauled Billy up and sat him down on a tree stump. He picked up Billy's trousers and pulled the thin leather strip out of the belt loops that Billy had been using to hold his trousers up. As Billy whimpered, the man pulled his wrists together and bound them with the leather strap. Then the man stood up straight and fisted his cock again.

"Open up, and you'd better suck it good, if you know what's good for you. No, just open wide, get your teeth and tongue out of the way, and I'll do the rest."

Billy gagged and his eyes were watering again, as, holding the sides of his head firmly in his hands, the red-headed assailant face-fucked Billy's mouth. He was enjoying it, throwing his head back and howling to the tops of the trees. Billy wasn't enjoying it very much. He had a hard time keeping his mouth passage open and breathing at the same time. But still, the danger of it, the wildness of not having control, had him aroused.

Billy made an attempt to escape again when the ruffian felt he was aroused enough to get on with it and pulled his dick out of Billy's mouth. Billy had gone soft again and wasn't liking this much now. There was no hope though. The man towered over Billy and was nimble. He got his hands on Billy's throat and Billy slowly went slack for him.

Thoroughly, cowed, Billy was on the small of his back on the tree stump, his bound arms over his head, the man holding his legs open and splayed out. Only a few inches of the cock were inside Billy, but he was a virgin and the man was huffing and puffing, finding it hard, but arousing progress. Billy was whimpering, beaten and subdued. The pain was washing over him in waves. But underneath that was his own arousal. He was going hard again.

The man pushed in deeper and Billy flinched and his pelvis jerked up, pulling the man in even farther. The ruffian laughed as Billy reached for his own cock, fully erect now, managing to fist it with both of his bound hands, and shot off up the man's heaving belly almost immediately.

"There, I told you you wanted it," the man said with a smile. He untied Billy's wrists, convinced that the young man was fully his now. "Now settle down and work with me."

Billy didn't want to "work with" this assaulter, but his body had a mind of its own. As the man bottomed and he started pumping Billy, Billy raised his pelvis to him and started an answering rhythm of his hips. There was little pain now. Just the pleasure of a man inside him, controlling him, wanting him, not giving him any choice in the matter. Billy reached under the man's shirt and moved his hands up to cover the man's muscular pecs. The man pulled Billy's legs in and, of his own accord Billy wrapped them around the small of the man's back and hooked his ankles together. The man laughed again and began pistoning harder.

"Oh, yes, you want it, you do. I read you right. A real prime little piece you are."

The man's hands freed, now, one went to one of Billy's nipples and the other to Billy's cock, pumping Billy hard again. The man pinched Billy's nipple, and the young man arched his back and moaned and licked his lips.

"Like it like that, do you?"

Seeing the effect it was having on Billy, the man moved both hands to Billy's nipples and started to cruelly pull and twist them. Billy writhed under him with pain-pleasure and began humping back at him hard. The ruffian stopped his fuck, letting Billy take over the pumping.

"Yes, yes. Punish me," Billy whimpered.

"Wanted it all along. Teasing me, you were," the man growled as he fucked. "Walkin' that stretch of the track, you were offering it. Just leading me on, maybe not wanting to give it to the likes of me. I should . . ."

The man was choking Billy with one hand and he'd pulled a knife out from somewhere and was brandishing it over Billy's face. Billy came again in a gush.

He collapsed and the man resumed his pumping, breathing hard, probably near ejaculation himself now. Billy's eyes followed the knife, moving down, toward his belly.

The man had asked him if he was going anywhere; if he was expected anywhere. In a flash of recognition, Billy's adrenalin kicked in. He gave a sideway's heave of his pelvis, sending the man off balance and causing him to slice into his own arm with the knife. The man gave a howl of pain and his attention went to his arm. Heaving out from underneath him, Billy lashed his leg out, kicking the man in the balls, and then he started running through the forest.

* * * *

All of this—not just the escape, but the thrill of what went before—was flashing through Billy's brain as he stood, three weeks later, watching Sam, the schoolmaster, chopping wood. Maybe it was the red hair that turned Billy's remembrance on to the ruffian with red hair and linked that with arousal. Whatever it was, standing there, watching Sam's muscles undulating and his red, shoulder-length hair, not pulled back now as it usually was, moving in the breeze and the motion of his chopping, naked to the waist, Sam felt himself going hard. He wanted him. He realized that's why he'd been coming around.

Before he'd started doing that, he'd passed this way by chance one day and heard strange sounds coming from Sam's cottage. It sounded like maybe the schoolmaster was in trouble. Billy had come to the open door and then shrank back in the shadows. The schoolmaster was fucking another man on his bed. The man was on his back, his legs spread and his knees bent. His feet were flat on the mattress but were lifting up on the balls and then lowering again on the heels in the rhythm of the fuck. The man's wrists were tied to the slats of the headboard above his head, and this may have been what Billy had found to be the most arousing.

The schoolmaster was kneeling between the man's legs, his knees under the other man's buttocks, lifting the man's pelvis to a cock that disappeared, lengthened, then disappeared, then lengthened, the red bush of the schoolmaster mingling with the golden bush of the other man at the downstroke. The schoolmaster's hands were gripping the other man's knees and moving his legs in and out in the rhythm of the fuck. When the man's knees were bowed out to the limit, Billy knew that the schoolmaster's cock was deep inside him. This is when the man would arch his back and moan deeply, followed by a sigh as his knees were brought closer together and the schoolmaster's buttocks pulled back. At various stages of the coupling, the schoolmaster's torso arched down so that the men's faces were mashed together and each tried to bury his tongue deep in the throat of the other.

"What is it that you want, Billy?" the schoolmaster suddenly asked, burying his ax head in a chunk of wood and looking directly at Billy. He was panting slightly.

Billy was panting slightly himself, his need and want painted on his face.

"Why is it you've been coming around? You don't need extra tutoring. You're already the smartest in the school and will be leaving within a month and going into an indenture with a printer, I hear. It's not schooling you want. I waste of a first-class mind, but I wasn't asked for my opinion. What is it then?"

Billy stood there mute for a moment and then he blurted it out. "I saw you with a man. There in your cottage. I know what you do."

"Is it that then, Billy?" Sam asked with a sigh. He hesitated for a moment and then he said, "Is that what you want from me, Billy—what the man you saw me with was getting from me?"

Billy stood mute, eyes cast down. But he didn't say no.

"Tell me, is it the cock you want? You must tell me."

Billy almost wavered then. It wasn't what he wanted to hear—that he must ask for it. He felt himself going soft. It couldn't be his decision. But, visions of those man's knees moving apart and together flooding his brain, he wanted it so badly that he gave a slight nod of his head.

The schoolmaster sighed again and pulled a wet rag out of a bucket of water beside him and rubbed it over his chest, the back of his neck, and into his armpits.

"You'd best come inside then," he said in a quiet voice. "You're of age now. I guess you can have a mind of your own. I can't say it isn't something I want too."

And then it wasn't Billy's decision anymore. Sam had moved across the yard to stand in front of Billy, His arms encircled Billy. Controlling him. His lips found Billy's and crushed them. Sam invading his mouth with his tongue. Billy opened to him, but he let Sam control the kiss. Billy felt himself going hard again. It was good now. It would be fine. Sam, taller, heavier, and more powerful than Billy, picked Billy up in his arms and slowly walked toward the cottage.

Billy was on his back on the bed, his legs spread, his knees bent, his feet flat on the mattress. Sam pushed his knees under Billy's buttocks, raising Billy's pelvis to him. The glans of Sam's cock was resting at the rim of Billy's pulsating entrance. Sam's fists gripped Billy's wrists, holding his arms up and to the sides as, his torso hovering over Billy's, Sam looked down into Billy's eyes.

"Please," Bill murmured.

"Please, what?"

"The strapping to the headboard. That too please. As I saw you do with—"

The schoolmaster looked exasperated. But after a brief pause, he said, "If you like," rose from the bed, came back with leather bindings that he used to strap Billy's wrists to the headboard, and resumed his position between Billy's thighs.

"It will hurt at first. But then it should be fine. I will be gentle."

Before Billy could respond, Sam had covered his lips with his own and was pushing inside with his tongue. Billy shuddered as Sam's cock pushed inside him an inch. Misunderstanding, Sam disengaged the kiss and lifted his head.

"Just a bit of pain. I promise."

"Please," Billy hissed. "Fuck me."

Sam lowered his face for a controlled kiss again, and Billy opened his mouth to him and flicked his own tongue inside

Sam's mouth. A few more inches, and Sam's cock head rested at Billy's prostrate. He rubbed there slowly, again and again. Billy's channel opened to him and Billy, still trapped by Sam's kiss, began to pant.

"Please, your hands. My knees."

Sam gave a low laugh, but he gripped Billy's knees in his hands and pushed the young man's legs apart as he slid deep inside him. He then slowly pulled out as he brought Billy's knees closer together.

Billy cried out and ejaculated. And then he thrust his pelvis hard up into Sam, taking Sam's cock deep inside him, thrusting again and again against Sam's cock.

Sam's head went up and he face took on a look of surprise. "You've done this before."

"Fuck me. Fuck me hard," Billy commanded and then he turned his face to the wall in frustration. He wriggled his buttocks and thrust again at Sam's pelvis, bringing the cock deeper inside.

Sam began to stroke in earnest. Deeper, harder, faster. Billy's own hips fought to keep up with him in the counterstrokes. The younger man's legs were being pumped back and forth at an increasingly faster pace. Sam was lost in the fuck, murmuring how sweet Billy was, how long he'd wanted to do this. Pledging his love, pumping in a frenzy, lost in the fuck.

"Yes. Fuck me. Punish me. Give it to me! Make me hurt!"

Sam went stiff and stopped stroking.

"What was that you said?"

"About what?"

"About punishing you?"

"I've been bad. I need your discipline. I am your misbehaving student, you prisoner."

Sam rolled off him and walked over to the mantelpiece and turned around. He looked achingly beautiful to Billy. And there was that red hair. Keeping the arousal alive. Still, Billy was confused and frustrated.

"How have you been bad, Billy?"

Billy was at a loss for words. The best he could do, after a moment of silence, was say. "Last month. I didn't come to school. I wasn't sick. It was just a nice day."

"Are you saying you don't want me to make love to you—that you want me to punish you? That you see sex with a man as justified punishment?"

Silence. After a bit, Sam continued, "I don't assault men, Billy. When they come to me, it's as equals. It isn't for me to punish or control them. They must want to fuck as equals. I make love, Billy. I don't rape. You asked for the binding. So did the man you saw me with. It isn't something I need."

There was nothing Billy could say. He suddenly felt naked and defeated.

"I think you'd best go now, Billy," Sam said as he came back to the bed and unbound Billy's wrists. "And you need not come back to class. You've learned more than enough. I hope you have learned this, now, too. Sex is good as equals, even between men. It is wrong if it must be taken from you. I hope that you will learn that someday. You are a highly desirable young man, Billy. I've wanted you since I came here as schoolmaster. But what you think you want, I can't give."

Sam then scooped up his trousers and left the cottage. He was chopping wood again, and didn't look up, when Billy left.

It hadn't taken Billy long to find men—older men—who would give him what put him into greater arousal. First the printer his father had unwittingly indentured him to—giving the man full control over Billy's life. Satisfying Billy's need to be fully controlled in the fuck. And also a businessman of the town, prominent, but with a secret that made Billy melt with want.

* * * *

Sitting in the wagon beside Ned on the headland north of Shernhaven, Billy was anxious to get on toward his goal. But first there was the fare to pay. While still kissing, Ned, first— Ned had to assert control and intent first—and then Billy, each unbuttoned the other and took the hand measure of each other's cocks. Although there was time, there wasn't a great deal, and

Billy wasn't doing this for pleasure, so he quickly bent over and lowered his mouth to Ned's engorging cock. The farmer's son leaned back in the wagon seat and moaned his pleasure as Billy, without complete success, tried to swallow the cock whole.

Ned fucked Billy from behind bent over the open tail of the wagon, as the horse snorted its desire to get on with the journey. In a shared interest to get on with it and over it, Billy wiggled his butt and used his channel muscles to massage not only great length out of Ned, but a fairly quick ejaculation as well. At Billy's request, Ned had pulled his arms straight away from the sides of his body and had bound his wrists to the wagon bed sidings with rope so that Billy was forcibly spread-eagled for the fucking.

For another fucking, Ned offered to pick Billy up here again on Sunday afternoon when the wagon would be heading for Boston again with produce for the Monday morning market, but Billy just thanked him and said he had other arrangements for a return to Boston. He did say, however, to Ned's delight, that perhaps they could repeat this arrangement at some point in the future.

After Ned drove off, happy and satiated, in his wagon, Billy walked carefully and quietly toward the largest of the house on the headland to the north of Shernhaven. He gave the house a wide berth. It was lit up with whale oil lamps as a demonstration of the wealth of the occupants, no doubt a purposeful message to the town below of the family's prominence. Walking along the edge of the cliff, he went into the far reaches of the garden, looking down, first, into the town through the masts of the ships in the boatyard at the base of the cliff to trace the passage he had to make, and then out to sea. There was more than one ship out there, at sea, toward the south, with lights twinkling. His mind was on two of the ships, both of which he prayed were out there. Having taken his bearings, Billy circuited around the house again and then strode out onto the lane that served all of the cliff-top houses of Shernhaven's leading citizens.

This was not a time for furtive movement now. Now he had to appear to belong here and to have someplace legitimate that he was heading to.

Two hours later, he had made his way down into the village, across it, and then up onto the headland defining the southern end of the harbor town. He walked openly toward the lighthouse, taking it as his beacon and as his goal should anyone ask. But when he got there, he faded into the underbrush just outside the cleared circle around the old lighthouse and, eventually, to the cliff overlooking the sea.

He had been here before, but it was still difficult to find a path that would safely lead him down into the sheltered coves at the edge of the sea and the base of the cliff. More than once he had to retrace his foot- and handholds, having followed a false path that led to a dead end and sheer drop to the churning surf below. The sounds of the waves and the seagulls wheeling overhead were mesmerizing. When he was sure he'd found a path he'd used before, he tarried for a moment and looked out to sea.

Two ships were standing off the coves at the base of cliff, near enough for Billy to see their white sails and to count their masts to assure himself that these must be the two ships he expected, but far enough out to sea not to run aground in this treacherous area of the coast. The ships weren't near each other. The larger of the two was between where he stood and the inlet leading past the lighthouse and into the Shernhaven harbor. The other one was standing further south.

Billy could see that the one farther away already had longboats in the water, starting their journey to land. They were carrying no running lights, but were merely dark splotches on the water, discerned in the moonlight only with great care. They were riding low in the water, and Billy could see a mass of figures overloading each one.

The nearer, larger ship, was just starting to lower boats. The sound of men calling out guidance and curses at the difficulty of the work slid in underneath the keening of the seagulls overhead and the pounding of the surf.

By the time Billy had made his way down to the cove and positioned himself behind a large boulder of water-pocked rock and jagged edges, boats from the two ships were nearing the beach. Their journey was intersecting on the beach nearly parallel to where Billy was hiding himself.

The longboats from the smaller, more distant ship, Billy could now see were packed with silent, dark figures. The boats from the larger ship were seemingly empty other than the men rowing, driven by a man growling curses and threatening slackers with bodily harm.

One of the overloaded boats foundered in the surf, and there was a scramble to pull its occupants, who didn't seem to be making much of an effort to save themselves, to safety. Billy could hear the ominous rattling of chains. The crews from the larger boats leaped out of their now-beached longboats and went to the aid of the other craft, a second of which was also foundering in the merciless surf. From the sounds of wailing from the floundering figures in the surf and the curses of the crew members, Billy could tell that not all of the passengers were being saved.

The coxswain of the larger ship's longboats seemed to have taken charge of the situation. He cut quite a figure in the late of the longboat lantern. He was dark—either heavily tanned or an Arab—and wore a bright green vest over short brown breeches. A scarlet sash circled his waist into which two pistols had been shoved. He was bearded and there was a black patch over one eye.

Billy knew how important it was to lose as few of the floundering passengers as possible. The figures were dark sinned and nearly naked. He knew that these would be slaves being brought in from Africa via the Caribbean. He was witnessing their transfer from one ship to the other and knew that by the morrow or the next day, the survivors of this landing would be displayed on the auction block on Woodman's wharf, near Boston's town market and docks. Those bidding on these slaves would be turning a blind eye to their primitive conditions and weakened, dazed states. In one of life's incongruities, whereas the trade of shipped slaves was now outlawed in Massachusetts, the resale of slaves in the state previous to the law's enactment was permitted. Those trading with these lives in the new day would be conveniently assuming the slaves hadn't arrived surreptitiously in the night.

So engrossed was Billy in watching the exchange of the goods, cases of rum and bolts of textiles and baskets of gleaming doubloons, from one ship for the slaves from another that he cried out in fear and surprise as a strong hand gripped his shoulder from behind.

"I believe you will be coming with us," a growly voice rang out.

Billy had been discovered by the commanding coxswain of the larger ship's longboats.

* * * *

A multitude of heavily callused hands backed by lustful grins, many of them nearly toothless and with suggestively winking eyes, pulled Billy up out of one longboat while a moaning ebony human cargo was handed up out of other longboats along the side of the great, black-wood ship. Billy looked up to the heavens at the sails already being unfurled for flight as the coxswain, with the help of two other burly and shirtless sailors, manhandled Billy across the deck. Those they passed whistled and leered and made rude sucking sounds with their mouths.

Billy was bustled through an arched door in the superstructure at the stern of the ship and down a corridor. The coxswain rapped on a sturdy door at the end of the gangway and listened for the summons from within. When it was given, Billy was propelled into a commodious cabin with large windows at the stern of the ship. The cabin was paneled in polished, dark wood. Oriental carpets covered the floor. Lighted sconces, covered with glass chimneys, were placed at intervals along the walls, revealing leather-backed and –seated arm chairs, heavy tables covered with maps and navigational tools, and, against one wall, a large four-poster bed.

In the center of the room was a tin bathtub, full of soapy water. And out of the water rose a giant of a man. He was well over six feet and heavily muscled from pecs to calves. He had dark, reddish hair, a rich auburn color with blondish-red highlights. The hair on his head was caught at the nape of his neck with a gold ring. The chest was broad and covered in curled auburn hair; he was deeply tanned; his waist, while thick, was made thus by plates of solid abdominal muscles rather than fat.

The thighs were heavily muscled, as were the calves; his biceps popped with pronounced curves; his forearms and the knuckles of his hands were covered with curly reddish-brown hair. Piercing black eyes bore into Billy as he was thrust into the room. The face was of chiseled angles, the nose hooked, but in a commanding way. His torso and thighs showed slash marks of numerous battles, but from the look of him, it was apparent that he didn't lose battles.

He stepped out of the tub, and Billy could see that the man's balls hung low and that his extraordinarily thick cock, which seemed of average length when he first stood in the tub, was now lengthening out alarmingly and was beginning to curve up toward his flat belly. His bush was a brighter red than the hair on his chest and head. Billy felt his breath stop, and he moaned.

"Look what we found on the beach, Bloody Jack," the coxswain said in an obsequious voice.

"Leave us." The voice was deep, commanding.

Billy quickly was alone with the giant. But not entirely alone. Off in the corner, relaxing on his haunches, lay a giant, black mastiff hound, which somehow perfectly mirrored in dangerous aspect the form of Bloody Jack. It looked on with curiosity, panting slightly, its eyes moving from its master to the interloper, as if wondering what will happen next, whether its services would be required.

The young captive stood, quaking, as the dominating figure, still dripping from the water in the tub, started walking toward him, stopped by a table and picked up a dagger, and then approached Billy and circled behind him, all the time devouring the younger, shuddering man with his eyes.

Suddenly, from behind, a meaty arm snaked between one of Billy's dangling arms and his torso and wrapped itself around Billy's chest, positioning a thick wrist beside the young man's neck and stronger fingers cupping his chin. Billy whimpered as the other hand started to cut his clothes away with the dagger.

The mastiff gave a low growl from across the room but settled down as soon as it realized who was the aggressor and who was the captive.

"Two months at sea only with gnarled sailors," the voice whispered in Billy's ear. "Not a single sweet ass among those we captured, and even those I rode could not last me. Two months without anything as nice as you. Feel free to fight me. I am going to fuck the fight out of you, boy."

Billy moaned and then cried out in pain and surprise as, naked now, his feet were lifted off the floor, his torso flipped forward as the giant released his chest hold, and an impossibly thick cock thrust inside him that began to pump him hard, pulling him back and forth rapidly on the cock. When he stopped, abruptly, Billy was gasping and shuddering.

"You like a pirate captain's cock, do you?" The man growled. Then he laughed.

As the man held a bent-forward Billy to him, with his cock buried in Billy's channel, the pirate captain slowly walked toward the center of the room, where the tub was. Billy's belly was pushed down onto the lip of the tub. His feet now found the floor, but the giant resumed pumping his ass. The man wound his arms under Billy's armpits, locked his fists at the nape of Billy's neck, and dipped Billy's head under the water in the tub. One, two, three, four thrusts of the cock, and then Billy's head was lifted free. He gasped and sputtered. And then under again. One, two, three, four thrusts. Up for air and a gasp and sputter and then under again.

Visions entered Billy's air-starved brain of the forest, bent over a stump. A red-headed ruffian brandishing a knife. Grinning and thrusting, thrusting, thrusting.

Billy was loose as a rag doll when the man hauled him up from the side of the tub, thrust him into one of the leather-backed and -seated arm chairs, high up the back, with his thighs hanging over the arms of the chair, rolled the younger man's pelvis up toward the thrusting angle of his cock and thrust and thrust and thrust.

After an eternity, he hauled Billy up from the chair, carried him over to the bed, tossed him into the middle of the bedding on his belly, landed on top of him with his knees on either side of Billy's thighs and rode the limp young man deep and hard like the stallion he was.

In the middle of the night, midst the sound of the waves being parted by the prow of the ship and the gentle snoring of the mastiff in the corner, whose name was Freedom, and the slight roll of the ship at sail, Billy woke with a whimper. An arm reached across his chest, and he was being gathered once more close into Bloody Jack's chest. Both were laying on their sides, and Billy could feel the power of the cock that had worked almost relentlessly inside him through the night pushing at the small of his back. He turned his face toward his assailant's and whispered. "Again, Ben, fuck me again. Hard. Punish me."

"Ah, I'm not as young as you are, Billy," Bloody Jack murmured. "How many times do you need the cock tonight?"

"Again and again. You said it. It's been two months. No one fucks me like you do."

"That's because I don't give it to you every night. If I did, you would soon grow tired of it."

"Never." There were several moments of silence punctuated by sighs and moans and the two let their hands work the body of the other. But then Billy raised an old request. "Take me with you the next time, Ben. I want to go to sea."

"No you don't, Billy. You are too good for that. You've seen the men out on deck. You don't want to become one of those. You are meant for greater things than that."

"What greater things?"

"Well, the right good sheath for my cock, for one thing."

They both laughed.

"And besides, you are too small and pretty to be a pirate."

Billy stiffened at this oft made remark concerning him, but he yielded as the pirate fondled him intimately with both hands. Shortly, Bloody Jack, having been rested and intimately handled by Billy, in turn, started claiming the sheath that was his again.

As they fucked, they felt the ship stop moving forward and coming to rest, followed by the scrape of the longboats on the ship's side and the murmurings and wailings of the slaves as they were brought up from below.

Billy knew they were north of Boston now, near yet another cove, where the slaves would be transported and then walked down into the city and prepared for the block.

"Why the short transfer?" Billy asked when Bloody Jack had spouted again and they were resting. "Why didn't the other ship take them to market?"

"He's not a member of the guild. He had to sell off shore. He couldn't sell in either Charleston or New Orleans either."

"Are you a member of the guild?"

"Not that one," he answered. Then he laughed. "But the slaver doesn't know that. I can double profits in a day."

"When do we dock?"

"In the morning."

"I don't have to be back at the printers until late Sunday afternoon."

"Good. I'll fuck you until you can't walk straight. All day tomorrow, here."

Billy sucked in is breath. "You know that's what I want. What legitimate goods do you have to offload to justify a two-month's sail from England."

"Fine furniture and porcelain."

"And what else? Beneath that—that you are offloading now with the slaves?"

"Booty. Four prizes this voyage. A little bit of everything, including Spanish doubloons."

"That's what I want. That's the adventure I want."

Ben snorted, and repeated the reservation he had given before."You are too small, lad, to be a pirate—and too pretty by far. The other pirates would all eat you alive." He paused there, though, and when he continued, he said, in a somewhat sadder voice. "But I can see that there is much of the call of the sea and of the freeboaters for you." Another pause. "I can give you all of the adventure you can handle. Do you see the dark object hanging from the center of the ceiling there?"

"Yes."

"Tomorrow at dawn, I hang you from there by both wrists and ankles, with your cock pointed at the deck, and I fuck the stuffing out of you."

Billy trembled at the sheer pleasure of the sound of that.

"So, rest now, my little bird. I want you to stay fully conscious for all I do to you tomorrow. We have so little time on this visit of mine to Boston."

A pirate. That's what Billy wanted to be. A pirate like Bloody Jack, who he knew as Ben. Not just like Bloody Jack, but alongside him. Plundering by day; being plundered by night.

The world thought that the age of pirates along the Atlantic coast of America was over, ended seventy-five years earlier with the hanging right here in Boston of William Fry, captain of *James' Revenge*. Now the loss of merchant ships was totted up to storms at sea, with all hands and goods going to the bottom of the Atlantic. But there were a few pirates still, like Bloody Jack and his *Black Falcon*, and though many a merchant ship and its crew were going to the bottom of the ocean, not all of their goods were experiencing that fate.

Billy sighed and drifted off to sleep, only to be awakened at dawn by rough hands pulling him up; trussing his wrists to his ankles, behind his back; being hoisted above the floor on the hook in the center of the cabin's ceiling at the level of Bloody Jack's pelvis, with the giant pushing in between his thighs, thrusting inside him, and pumping hard. Blood Jack always kept his promises.

"Yes, Yes! Oh fuck, yes, Punish me!"

* * * *

Two weeks later William Evan's Senior was giving a dinner for a leading citizen of Boston, a rum distiller and textile manufacturer, on a Sunday evening and wanted to show his son off. He wanted to do business with the important manufacturer and wanted him to see that his business was stable—that he had a son to pass it on to. It didn't matter that he had little hope that his worrisome son would follow in his footsteps. But the businessman need not know that.

The printer, Henry Gawn, was quite pleased to permit Billy to go to the dinner. He could see printing consignment possibilities with both Mr. Evans and Mr. Palmer, and anything that Billy could do to help make that happen would be beneficial.

"Even if you have to bed the man to influence him. Or bed your father, for that matter," Henry said.

Billy just gave him a watery smile.

During the dinner, Billy and Mr. Palmer barely spoke, but Palmer did seem to be interested in possible business ventures with the older Evans. The discussions went late. Henry had given Billy permission to sleep at home that night, but he still had to be back at the printer's shortly after dawn on Monday morning.

Thus, Billy, along with his mother and sisters excused himself, leaving the two businessmen still sitting at the dining table and smoking pipes and sipping on watered-down rum. Billy went to his room on the top floor, stripped, and pulled on his night shirt. Then he went out into the hall and sat on the floor, his back against the wall, beside the staircase, and listened to the conversation below.

Not long after that, William Senior let Mr. Palmer out of the front door, snuffed the candles, and came to his own bedroom two flights below where Billy was crouched. Billy counted the minutes until the house was silent except for his father's familiar deep snore. Then he crept down the stairs, to the front door, silently unlocked and opened the door, and let Mr. Palmer back in.

Back in Billy's bedroom, Mr. Palmer pulled Billy's night shirt over his head, roughly pushed him down on his back on the edge of the bed, hurriedly unbuttoned the fly of his trousers, grabbed and spread Billy's legs, and thrust a hard, throbbing cock inside him.

"I didn't think I'd get through dinner without needing to get my cock inside you."

"Oh, god, yes, Ben," Billy growled. "Fuck me hard and deep. Yes, just like that."

Benjamin Palmer, leading Boston citizen, rum distiller and textile manufacturer—and, not incidentally, the Atlantic coast pirate known as Bloody Jack—fucked Billy desperately, as if it had been months, not weeks since they last had coupled.

Being awakened by muted but unfamiliar sounds as well as the incongruous sound of slapping, flesh on flesh, William Evans Senior crept out of bed, quietly mounted the two flights

30

of stairs to the fourth floor, and stood outside Billy's bedroom door. The door was open enough for him to see the two men fucking—and to identify who they were. Ben Palmer was fucking Billy like a dog, bent over his bed, and was fisting Billy's head hair with one hand, arcing Billy's torso cruelly back toward him, and slapping Billy's buttocks hard with the palm of his other hand with each thrust of his cock, so lost in lust that he gave no heed to the pistol shot-like sound of the slaps in the confines of the small attic bedroom.

He might have intervened if the sounds Billy was making didn't indicate that Billy was enjoying the assault and if he didn't need Palmer's business and if he had never found his son thus occupied before. With a shrug and a second—and third—look, followed by a guilt-filled shake of his head, he descended the stairs and went back to bed.

However, on the morrow, he took pen to paper and wrote his brother-in-law, Charles Rawley, with the proposal that Billy be sent to him to work on his rice plantation in South Carolina—the harder the work the better.

Chapter Two:

Charleston, 1802

Young Billy landed in Charleston, South Carolina, by ship, at his uncle's own wharf, Brown's wharf, at the Cooper River foot of Queen Street. He was surprised to find that it was a lot warmer in Charleston in late October than it was in Massachusetts. And after coming from the more staid Boston, he was also taken with the frivolity he found here; it was the beginning of the social season in the city.

His mother's brother, Charles Rawley, both a rice planter and a slave auctioneer, was one of the busiest businessmen of the city. He was a wealthy man, thanks to his two ships plying between Charleston, loaded with rice, to market in either Alexandria, Egypt, to be loaded there with slaves for the needs of the New World, or Boston to exchange rice and indigo for finished textiles and rum. It was one of these ships that had transported Billy. He had thoroughly enjoyed the sail, convincing the captain to let him apprentice as a sailor and learn the rudiments of the ship.

In return for the attention the captain had given him, Billy let the man play his channel with his cock. It wasn't just pirates who fucked other men on sea voyages, Billy learned. It was a proclivity of merchant sailors too, there not being many woman on a ship during long voyages. Now Billy was more sure than ever that he wanted a life before the mast—and being taken roughly with sailors' masts.

Billy had been met on the dock by the manager of his uncle's counting house, being told that the Rawleys were at church. The manager managed to convey to Billy that Charles Rawley was very religious and nothing came before that in his family's life. Billy was immediately unsure how he was going to fit in here.

Charles Rawley's star was on the rise, and he had just this year, 1802, taken possession of his newly constructed townhouse at 24 Queen Street.

It wasn't a large house, certainly not to the standards of the house on Rawley Place plantation fifteen miles up the Ashley River, but as the family only resided in Charleston during the winter, social season months, it was quite adequate for Rawley and his wife and two teenage daughters.

Now, however, he had to make do with his troubled nephew from Boston. Billy's father had bought out his son's indenture to the printer, Henry Gawn, much to the latter's consternation, and had given it to Rawley in exchange for Rawley putting up with a recalcitrant young man of unspeakable proclivities that his own father couldn't countenance. Of course, William Senior hadn't told Charles what those circumstances were—only that the son needed discipline, close supervision, greater contact with the church, and to be somewhere else other than Boston.

In his letter to his brother-in-law, William Senior had strongly suggested that Billy be put to work on the Rawley plantation, with no burden spared. Charles Rawley had taken this suggestion with more than a grain of salt, knowing that his Boston relatives had no idea how rigorous plantation life was for a cultivator of rice. That was why they enslaved natives from Africa for the work. No, he wouldn't send Billy to the plantation. He would use him, making stock tallies, in the company counting house at the foot of Queen Street. When he saw the young man in the flesh, he was convinced that he had been right. Billy was small of stature and much too handsome to be working in the fields. He was muscular enough, having been worked hard at the printing trade, but he was more slender and boyish looking than the planters and overseers who closely supervised the working of the fields. He didn't look like someone who keep slave laborers in line.

Dressed well, which was one of the first orders of business, Charles thought, Billy would be quite popular in Charleston during the social season, though. All of the eligible young ladies would be buzzing around him, putting their fathers in a position to talk business with Charles. Charles even regretted somewhat that his own daughters were Billy's cousins and therefore not eligible for the hunt.

As far as supervising Billy, he would give the lad space in the attic of his new town house to sleep and otherwise would occupy his time with work so heavy that he would have no chance to roam to engage in whatever mischief had gotten him shipped south. But he would keep a tight rein on Billy. An indenture was an indenture, and Charles Rawley, like all of the other Southern planters, knew what it meant to own the work of another human being—what the balance was between the profit they brought in and the cost of their upkeep.

If Billy had been consulted—which he hadn't been—he likely would have asked what the difference was between being enslaved and indentured—other than the color of the skin of the man being subjected to the control. Total sexual control as from the pirate Benjamin Palmer, and total control over everything a man did were two different matters to Billy. He had his majority; he was approaching the age of nineteen. And his family was not poor. Why should he be controlled by any other person as tightly as an African slave was?

Life became full for Billy that winter, just as his father had planned and his uncle was providing. He was worked hard in the counting house and walked the three blocks to his uncle's townhouse more often than not after dark either to be locked in for the night or, on rare occasion, to go out for the evening with his uncle at Rawley's gentlemen's club, Cooper's. Cooper's was housed in a townhouse residence tucked discretely on the short Orange Street, one block south of King Street, which served as a backbone to the oval-shaped peninsula jutting out toward sea between the mouths of the Ashley and Cooper rivers.

Here, Billy would sit behind his uncle and watch him at his major passion, gambling games, mostly poker, before the two were escorted upstairs to be treated each to a fuck with a young woman at Rawley's expense. Billy dutifully performed and, in fact, was a favorite of the young ladies of the club, but his heart was not in it. He just knew that it would not be in his interest for his uncle to become more the wiser about what Billy preferred. He knew that his uncle sometimes watched through a peephole to gauge how virile and expert his nephew was, the capability to perform and breed being as important in the pedigree of a prospective bridegroom in the Southern plantation class as it was to the value of a stud horse. Billy made sure his uncle wasn't disappointed in what he saw—nor were the young women he was with. As handsome as he was, he'd had considerable opportunities to lay with woman before he discovered his preference for men.

Nearly all of the gentlemen planters with city residences belonged to such a club. Not many belonged to one as exclusive as Cooper's, though. In the spring and fall seasons they were at their upriver plantations and had a mulatto slave woman—or young man or boy—or two to provide variety to the attentions of their wives. Here in Charleston, they had their clubs. There were plenty of prostitutes on the streets for those of lesser status, but they, of course, were not the cream of the crop that the clubs provided.

Billy got to know the men frequenting Cooper's very well, as it was a select group. Prominent among them was the Episcopalian rector of St. Michael's church, only two blocks north of the club at the corner of Meeting and Broad. Billy saw the Reverend Andrew Apsley regularly at church and midweek services, as well, because Uncle Charles was taking William Senior's plea of Billy's increased attachment with the church very seriously. William was of the same mind as many that Billy could be "cured" by turning to religion.

Reverend Apsley was an avid gambler, and he never could resist a high-stakes poker game at the club. Billy would watch the tall, gaunt man, with fascination, sitting there in his pious black cassock and clerical collar, knocking back his rum, and knitting his thick, gray-speckled eyebrows. He was constantly gazing intently at those holding the other hands under his hooded eyelids and pursing his thick lips in a knowing "my

God is sitting on your shoulder and telling me what cards you hold" manner. He didn't often lose. He left the definite impression that he didn't lose well. Among his other vices were the brown Virginia tobacco cigarettes he chain-smoked and the superior attitude he took with all. Decidedly not among his bad habits, though, was that he never went upstairs to fuck the young girls.

He didn't converse with Billy except for the moments of leaving on the steps of the church after Sunday and midweek services, but Billy had the impression when he visited Cooper's with his uncle that the Reverend Apsley was ever aware of where he was, what he had said, and what he had done. Billy was just grateful that his uncle wasn't a Catholic and that Episcopalians didn't have confessional requirements.

Cooper's was not Billy's only chance to have sex with women that winter. His eldest cousin, Elizabeth, was very taken by him and showed every indication that he could take liberties with her if he wished—and his aunt, Charles's wife, showed every indication that she wouldn't mind a forced marriage between the two, regardless of the inbreeding taboos. Her family was from the mountains to the west, and in their somewhat more isolated and primitive conditions, cousin marrying cousin was not unheard of—or disapproved of.

Billy didn't wish such an arrangement, however, and he politely held his cousin at arm's length without doing her the insult of revealing that he preferred the cocks of men. He was less polite with the wife of the manager of the counting house who visited with special treats for the men several times during that winter and would have raped Billy behind bales of wool if he hadn't been nimble at staying at least one step out of her grasp.

There, of course, were no opportunities—at least for Billy's initial months in Charleston—to fuck men. There were balls nearly every Friday or Saturday night that were as exhausting as they were boring for Billy. Saturdays and Sunday afternoons were taken up with either visiting or being visited, with the entire Rawley family decked out in expensive clothes and transported around the city in an open town carriage. There were men during these visitations that Billy thought were strongly attracted to him, but he and they were never left alone. And one young woman or another was constantly being thrust at him.

It was in otherwise innocuous conversations during these visitations, though, that Billy began to see a glimmer of hope for an easing of the gilded cage he was being imprisoned in. A common thread ran through the chit-chat from men who gravitated to him during family visitations but who were as restricted in what they could say and do in this context as Billy was. He noticed that such men invariably would ask him what he was doing after the season—in the spring. Would he be staying in the city or going to Rawley Place plantation with the rest of the family?

Invariably Billy would say that that was up to his uncle, as he, Billy, was indentured to him. He noticed, however, that the men's eyes would light up and a little smile would flick across their faces when he added that, as he was gathering increasing responsibilities in the counting house, it was likely that he would be staying in the city.

It didn't take him long to see this as his opportunity for increased freedom. If the rest of the family was fifteen miles upriver and only he and the town servants were at 24 Queen Street, who was there to tell him when he could come and go— and where he could go? There were servants in the house, certainly, but they were as much enslaved as he was. He was sure he could loosen his leash by loosening theirs as well, and that no one need be the wiser.

This is exactly what transpired. During the waning weeks of winter, Billy did all he could to make himself indispensable at the counting house, thus making Charles's decision to leave him in the city a natural one that Charles could come up with himself.

There was nothing Billy wouldn't do at the counting house—except for having anything to do with the sale of the African slaves taken straight off his uncle's ships and sold on a block standing at the land side of Brown's wharf right beside the counting house.

The first time he had been asked to stand by and tally up the bids, he had been traumatized by the wretchedness of the creatures being sold. The one exception was a big, strapping warrior of a man, heavily muscled and his magnificent body and face pocked with blue tattooing. The man stood tall and straight and glowered with superiority and ferocity at any and all who came close to him. He bared his teeth and pounded his chest, making his chains rattle, at the mere audacity of the clerk standing next to Billy to suggest the opening of a bid. He looked murderously at any and all who opened their mouths to speak, and his gaze ended on Billy. Naked hatred and belligerence. The look of "I could and would tear you apart with my hands, given the chance," sent a chill down Billy's back.

What was startling, though, was that it was a shudder of sensuality. Billy knew that he melted to being dominated and abused by a powerful man—it was what made him a moth to the flame that was the pirate Benjamin Palmer. He was afraid of this giant of an ebony captive, yes. But at the same time he ached to be taken by one such as him. He'd never lain with a black man before. This one was naked and his manhood, in partial erection, was humbling to any other man on the wharf.

In the ensuing weeks, Billy often wondered in the night how it would be to be taken roughly by a black man—especially one as hugely endowed as this tattooed slave was.

There was no bid. All were instantly cowed by the ebony giant. In the end, he was sent in chains to Rawley Place to work in the rice fields if and as he could be broken down to do so. If he couldn't, he probably would have to be put down, the manager of the counting house told Billy.

The experience was more traumatic than Billy wanted to face again, though. The thought of such a magnificent creature being put down simply because he wanted to stand as tall as a man in the New World as he had done in his African kingdom was repugnant to Billy, who had not grown up in the South, and thus had not inherently learned that black men were counted as less than human. After that, Billy made sure he had duties to perform inside the counting house when the slave auctions on Brown's Wharf were in train.

What he found to do, though, was valuable enough to the Rawley fortunes that, expressing his regrets, Uncle Charles

38

told Billy it would be best if he remained at work in the city during the spring.

Billy did what he could to show a slight pique at this imposition, making his uncle express regret that this burden was being laid on his young nephew's shoulders.

* * * *

Less than a week after the Rawley family bustled its way out of Charleston, baggage carts in train, to open up the big house at Rawley Place, Billy was starting a new, but subtly different schedule. He appeared to be working at the counting house hours longer than he had been before, often not getting back to 24 Queen Street until the early hours of the morning, only to have to rise again shortly after dawn to return to work.

He was happier now, though. And this was primarily because he wasn't coming straight back to the Queen Street townhouse from the nearby counting house. Instead, he was making a detour to the Prioleau Wharf area farther out on the city peninsula and, more precisely, to the Elliott Street waterfront. This was the rough and tumble quarter of the city that was given over to the common sailors who were in port and who were exploding with freedom and whatever cash they had accumulated that they had not been able to turn into liquor or sex for the months they'd been at sea before docking at the major port of Charleston.

It wasn't just common sailors who gladly departed ship in Charleston to carouse. Piracy was still booming in the Caribbean, and Charleston was about as far north as their ships and crew would come on the North American continent to exchange their loot for booze and services. A Charleston that was prim and proper on the surface, but hedonist just below that thin veneer, was as happy to take golden Spanish coins from pirates as from any staid merchantman.

Billy felt free and alive just to be mingling with these rough sailors. He wasn't as large and menacing as those he tended to gravitate to, but he was nimble and smarter by far than any of them, and he was good at picking out men who wanted to give him what he wanted. On the average of twice a week, Billy allowed one of them, usually the biggest bruiser of the lot, to take him into a back room or an alley and fuck him rough and hard. This was beginning, at least, to scratch an itch that had been plaguing Billy ever since he'd been shipped south. He considered it something temporary—just to take the edge off his need. What he didn't realize was that he was picking out men with an increasing aura of danger and meanness.

He realized—but too late, the mistake he was making one drizzly night in an alley opening some twenty feet away onto Edgar's North Wharf, the roughest part of the quarter. He had sat in the lap of a grizzled pirate who was fairly well hacked up from barroom brawls and ship attacks and had felt enough of the prodigious equipment and need of the man to want him inside him. He had whispered his own immediate want in one of the man's cauliflowered ears and been unceremoniously hustled out a side door of the boisterous bar and into the alley. Billy's trousers had been ripped away, and the bruiser had produced a sharp knife in one hand and was mashing Billy's face into a dirty brick wall with the other as he clumsily poked at Billy's hole with the bulb of his cock.

Billy thought this was getting more out of hand than he wanted—especially with the appearance of the knife, which had already nicked him under the chin and was causing blood to flow. He tried to spin out of the man's grip and run off, but the pirate was too strong for him. The knife slashed across Billy's arm and he collapsed into concern for that wound, while the bruiser lifted him with hands gripping his waist and settled him down on a thick cock.

The man held Billy fast to him with one arm slanted up the smaller man's torso and a fist gripping Billy's chin. The other hand held the knife pointed up, with the tip nicking Billy just under his rib cage on the left side.

"Settle down and enjoy the fuck of your life," the pirate hissed.

Billy did that, now being on familiar ground that gave him a buzz. He raised his feet off the ground and wrapped them back around the pirate's hairy legs so that his feet could hook on the top of the man's heavily muscled thighs.

The pirate began the long, deep rhythm of the fuck. This was what Billy had come for. But he was concerned about that knife. It was pressing into him below his rib cage, and he felt like he was continually moving uphill trying to get out of it's painful touch.

"Do you know what's just above the point of this knife?" The man growled in Billy's ear. And then, before Billy could respond in any fashion, the pirate continued, "It's your heart. This is how I best like to take a man. This is your last fuck, so enjoy it."

Billy moaned, fully getting the drift of what was happening here. He involuntarily flinched then as the cock drove unusually deep, and cried out as the knife point pushed in, going a bit farther in than just breaking the skin.

"You'll be wanting to hold still for as long as possible. It's gonna happen, but you'll enjoy it more and longer if you hold still. This is what's gonna happen. I want you to know. I want you to count the seconds left in your life by how good my staying power is. As I jack off inside you, the knife's going up into your heart. A new fuckin' meaning of a good death. You'll want to keep me from shooting off for as long as possible, but you'll love your last second almost as much as I do."

Billy moaned again. But it was a rush for him too. He was hard as a rock too. There was nothing he could do about this. This was as high as it got for him in arousal.

He felt the man stiffen and knew that he was about to blow. "Chrisalmighty, you got a sweet ass. I'm gonna . . ."

Billy held his breath, poised for the fatal thrust . . . taking him into chaos as he had the sense that the dogs of hell were churning up his world.

* * * *

"It was only one dog. Freedom over there," Ben Palmer responded to the first question Billy asked when he came to. Billy looked toward the corner of the captain's cabin on the *Black Falcon*, where the coxswain from the beach at Shernhaven crouched beside Ben's big, black mastiff and petted the dog. The dog was panting with his mouth hanging open, obviously enjoying the attention.

Billy could feel the cock slowly working his insides and he looked down his belly. Ben was standing between his legs, with Billy's ankles propped up on his shoulders, fully encased and fucking him in slow pumps.

"Sorry, I couldn't wait for you to come to," Ben murmured. "It's been months."

The younger man sighed and lifted a hand to place it on Ben's bulging breast, but Ben gently pushed it aside. "Not until we have these cuts taken care of." He was washing Billy's cuts and applying clean strips of cloth. His cock kept moving slowly inside Billy's channel, though, and Billy rolled his pelvis up to get the full benefit of the long slide.

"What . . . ?" Billy began.

"Nob there was in the same bar you were in. I let him take Freedom with him so the dog could get some firm land to piss on. He knew what that bastard you went with liked to do with boys, and so he followed you out into the alley and intervened when the sex got rough. He sicced Freedom on the son-of-a-bitch. Between the dog and Nob using the man's own knife on him, he won't be having his special thrill anymore."

"Ben . . ."

"What?"

"I'm scared."

"Why's that? You're safe now."

"I'm scared because it gave me a rush. I don't want to be safe. It's the scare that turns me on high."

"I know. I know that about you. It gives me a rush too. But it isn't healthy. For you, it isn't healthy. For me, fucking a tight little ass almost to death is just fine."

"Ben . . . I need you to fuck me nasty."

"Billy, you know I'm not jealous of you with other men, don't you? And you know I try to give you what you want."

"Yes."

"Nob over there saved you. And he's got a surprise I think you'd like. I'll give you what you asked for now. But he would like to watch."

"OK," Billy answered after a pause. He felt himself on the rise, so he did guess he liked that idea.

"And then I'm going to give you to Nob for half the night," Ben said in a low voice.

Billy moaned, but felt himself going harder.

"And then he's going to give you to the rest of the men in the forecastle for the rest of the night. Some of them are very rough and haven't had sex in a while. I haven't let all of the men go ashore yet."

Ben turned his face from Billy so that the younger man couldn't see how sad this made him. He wanted the best experiences for Billy—he knew that that was what turned him on—but he was afraid Billy would go too far, as he almost had done earlier tonight. It was a sacrifice to give him to the men, but he'd give them instructions. Billy would be returned to him alive—and in good enough condition for Ben to get what he wanted out of the relationship too.

"Oh, god, Ben." Billy felt himself going weak, all of his blood going to his dick. But he didn't have time to react further. Ben had grabbed his throat with both of his hands and was squeezing the breath out of Billy while at the same time slamming him hard, again and again, with his cock.

One, two, three, four thrusts, and the grip on his throat was released. Billy coughed and sucked in air. Ben tightened his grip again and Billy's eyes bugged out. His cock was at full staff though, and was beginning to ooze precum. One, two, three, four, thrusts. Then release and gasp. Pressure. One, two . . .

Billy was still gasping for breath as Nob lifted him up, slung him over his shoulder and left the captain's cabin. The coxswain sang out what was in the offing—sweet tail for the taking—as he strode down the deck toward the forecastle, and the crew, with hoots and whistles began to gather around.

Nob's secret—and, no doubt the origin of his name— was a thick but stubby cock that looked like it couldn't do a thing inside a man but that, when given entry, grew in both length and girth and had Billy gasping as Nob fucked and pumped the young man's cock hard to ejaculation.

And then it was a multitude of grinning faces and naked men and wagging cocks in erection or getting there fast. Billy writhed and moaned and groaned and grunted and shouted out at the continuous taking until dawn.

Back in the captain's bed in the early morning, Billy was laying on his back on the bed, one ankle on Ben's shoulder as the pirate captain sat on the edge of the bed below him.

"That's three," Ben murmured. "I got these in Egypt. I was told they are called Persian Delight."

Billy was holding very still, reveling in the three porcelain balls on a string that were inside his channel. There were three to go.

"Ben, you don't really mind. About last night."

"No, you told me what you needed. I gave you what I could. Don't ask me to snuff out your life during sex, though. That would snuff out my life as well."

"Ben . . ."

"Yes. Four . . . and five. God have you been stretched. You need some rest to get that back to tight enough for me to be interested."

Billy twitched and moaned. "Take me with you this time. I want to go to sea."

"You want smelly, ugly men fucking you night and day?"

"That too. Ugh." The sixth porcelain ball was inside him. "But I want to be one of you. I want the danger. Of being a pirate."

"Not today. But maybe tomorrow. Be at your family's pier at dawn and . . . maybe."

Billy sighed, reaching out for Ben. But Ben was standing now.

"And, are you ready for this, Billy." Ben grabbed Billy's ankles, wishboned his legs, and started working his cock inside Billy's channel behind the six porcelain balls in there.

Billy arched his back and cried out in frightened pleasure.

Freedom, laying in the corner, whimpered, and covered his eyes with a paw.

* * * *

Billy stood at the end of the wharf for hours the next day, looking out toward the sea, willing the sails of the *Black*

44

Falcon to be there. But to no avail. Several times men from the counting house came out to ask him what the matter was, but he just shrugged them off.

He should have known. Ben had given in too easily. Would there ever be a way that both he and Ben could get what they wanted out of each other and for both to be happy? He had no idea.

That night, he dressed in elegant clothes and walked the four and a half blocks across town to Orange Street and Cooper's gentlemen club. He knew that he would find what he wanted, what he needed, there.

He arrived late in the evening, knowing that most of the patrons would be gone—but that the one patron he sought would be there.

The Reverend Andrew Apsley was just moving from the gaming room to the gentlemen's lounge for a late snifter of port and a few more of his special Virginia tobacco cigarettes. But he stopped dead in his tracks in the entrance from the front hall into the lounge when Billy entered the front hallway and the doorman had evaporated to wherever the servants disappeared when they sensed their presence wasn't wanted.

The rector stood tall and gaunt, looking like an avenging angel in his black cassock with the slice of white high collar at his neck. His eyes burnt like black coals, boring into Billy. His thick lips puckered into a slight scowl.

Billy sensed that the minister was going to admonish him for not attending church services at St. Michael's since the Rawleys had left for their plantation. But that wasn't what Billy had come for. He had come for something far more dangerous. He knew he wasn't wrong. In the weeks he had watched Apsley—and especially how Apsley had watched him—Billy knew he wasn't wrong. And, more important, he knew that Apsley would be relentless and cruel.

"I came to play poker, but I have no stakes to offer," Billy said.

"You have assets far more valuable than money," Apsley answered. His voice was like a whip crack. Billy moaned, knowing that it had already begun.

After Billy lost at poker, which he knew he would, Apsley returned to the lounge and ordered his port. After the servant had vanished, Apsley sat in a wing chair, his legs spread, and Billy knelt before him, going up underneath the cassock, and finding the man naked underneath. His cock was erect, curling up cruelly. There was a fat silver ring piercing the glans, a style Billy had heard was becoming popular on the docks of Marseilles but that he shuddered in pleasure to find on this man of the cloth. Billy wasn't surprised at the nakedness or the obvious preference, though. In those earlier visits, he had noted that the reverend never went upstairs with the girls, but that he often left with a young man. Billy never had seen any of these young men again. The mere thought of the possible implications of those factors had Billy trembling with arousal.

Billy began to suck the man's cock underneath the cassock, reveling in the danger of the act, knowing that another guest could walk in on them at any moment.

He gasped and gagged and then one of his hands went to the buttons of his own trousers and then to his hardening cock, as Apsley grabbed his head through the fabric of the cassock and held it in place and he began thrusting his pelvis up, pushing his cock to the back of Billy's throat until he came and Billy sputtered his surrender.

The church's rectory was in St. Michael's Alley at the side of the church itself. The objects Aspley had gathered in the basement of the house were ones he told anyone who asked had been collected for a museum of the Catholic Church's Inquisition period.

The rack he tied a naked Billy to was one where Billy's belly was folded over a saddle affair on a trestle and his legs were tied in a wide stance to legs of the machine. His arms were stretched out wide at either side and tied down on wings extending from the central structure. It was a simple device really, and it held Billy bent over, with his head hanging down toward the floor, quite effectively and completely.

Billy cried out in ecstasy at the glorious never-before-experienced pain of the whip lashings of his back and thighs and buttocks followed by the paddling of his exposed and sore buttocks cheeks.

The fucking was fast, hard, and cruel, with Apsley grabbing the hair on the back of Billy's head and arching his torso back. Billy concentrated on the effect of the thick silver ring inside him and, as he ejaculated for the second time since he'd been on the rack, he knew he'd made the right decision to seek Apsley out.

When Apsley crouched down in front of him, smiled up into his face, and moved his lit cigarette toward Billy's nipple, the young man's eyes went wide, his adrenalin spiked, and his moan arced into a scream.

Over the course of the spring and summer, Billy visited Apsley's basement more than six times. It was obvious that the clergyman was fond of the young man, if for no other reason than that Billy was permitted to leave the dungeon room in order to return that many times. For the danger of it, Apsley also took Billy out to Sullivan's Island to the north of the city to observe a cock fight. Billy sucked Apsley off as they sat in the back of Apsley's carriage with the top pulled up enough to put them into the shadows as Apsley watched the cock fighting and licked his lips. Apsley continued to watch the cocks tearing each other apart even while Billy was perched in the clergyman's lap and riding his cock.

If any of the other patrons watching the event also watched the debauchery in Apsley's carriage, nothing was said in public. Soon thereafter, though, Billy started to have "chance encounters" and suggestions of assignations from some of the men he had met in their homes during the social season who, through some excuse or another, had found they had business that needed to performed in the city, away from their plantations, and who had, hopefully, it was evident, asked him if he would remain in the city after the social season was over and his uncle had retreated to his own plantation.

Such encounters were numerous enough that rumors began to seep out—and then to fly.

When Charles Rawley returned unexpectedly during the fall harvesting of the rice on his plantation, lured back by the rumors, he found Billy tied to the four-poster bed in the master bedroom of the Queen Street townhouse and being fist fucked by a half-drunk sailor.

A week later, Rawley now fully aware of why his brother-in-law had sent Billy south, bundled Billy off to the Rawley Place plantation with instructions of his own that paralleled William Senior's earlier request that Billy be put at hard labor and closely supervised—and the Rawley women were brought back to Charleston weeks ahead of the start of the 1803 social season.

* * * *

Rice planting was among the most human-labor intensive and demanding of cultivations. Conducted in river marshes of hot, humid, mosquito-infested locations, the crops had to be closely developed and maintained, with individual attention to individual plants, over a seven-month period stretching from late March to September. The fields were drained of water and the seed was sown by hand. The fields were flooded for a week to water the seeds and then drained again. The plants had to be weeded—also by hand—so the fields were periodically drained, and the workers moved from plant to plant in the soggy soil, weeding out all but the rice plants. Then the fields were flooded again to give the plants the continuous moisture then needed to grow. This cycle went on periodically through the late spring and hot summer months. The constant flooding and draining took a heavy toll on the banks of the fields, so these had to be monitored and repaired constantly. When the rice plants were harvested in September after the final draining of the fields for the season, the rice kernels had to be beaten out of the stalks, hulled, and then polished for packing—all by hand—loaded on boats, and floated down the river to the city from which the rice was then transported to its final market.

Billy arrived at Rawley Place, escorted by the plantation's hard-driving overseer, Hammond, during the last weeding of the drained fields before the last flooding. This was perhaps the most labor-intensive weeding period and the process had done its worst to the banks. In keeping with Charles Rawley's instructions, Billy was immediately sent among the slaves weeding the fields, and when he had become fully adept at doing this, he was turned over to the crew repairing a levee in the lowest field. Every member of this crew was a strong male slave, those with the most developed musculatures, as the work was the hardest.

To Billy's consternation—and his arousal, as well—the defiant ebony giant he had seen go unsold on the block at Brown's Wharf earlier in the year because of his belligerent and unyielding nature, was a member of this crew. The other black men were hunks, as well, but this one man was the dominator. All of the rest acceded to his direction.

His attitude had not changed appreciably. When Hammond brought Billy forward and told the crew that Billy was to receive no special consideration and was to be worked hard, Billy saw the gleam in the eye of the ebony giant, who was introduced to him as Spear. A good name, Billy thought, having seen the man's spear on the auction block. He was wearing short leggings held up with a rope now—as were all of the men, including now Billy, with Spear's showing a particularly prominent mound at his groin.

Hammond told the men that, although a member of the plantation owner's family, Billy would be staying in the overseer's house with him. Billy saw that this statement had an unusual effect on the men, who exchanged secret smiles and some sneers. Billy found out that very night why this was so. Hammond lived alone, he knew of the rumors of why Billy was there, he fucked men, and Billy was totally under his control.

At the base, Hammond was a primitive man. He was stronger than he looked, being gaunt and wiry. There was no fat on him. He was all muscle, with the veins of his arms popping out because they had no fatty tissue to travel through. He had to be strong to manage the slaves, although there were several underseers to help him. He walked with a bull whip that he knew well how to use. He didn't use a whip on Billy, though. He didn't need too. He was so hard-bodied and hard-minded that he could do whatever he wished and Billy knew that he could.

He didn't have to use any coercion. He simply told Billy at bedtime what he wanted from him and pulled his night shirt over his head. Billy sank to his knees in front the naked overseer and gave him the preparation and the incentive he demanded. Then he pulled Billy's night shirt over his head and motioned toward the bed. As Billy reached the bed, Hammond approached him from the rear and bent Billy over the bed, with Billy's hands planted in the mattress and his feet on the floor.

Hammond was a man of routine. Every night Billy was with him, he wanted the buildup to ejaculation the same way—in four positions, all basic. Nothing inventive about Hammond. It started that first night as it would every subsequent time, with Hammond wrapping an arm around Billy's bent body from the back and fucking him in a set rhythm of two shallow and one deep and then repeat. Then he wanted Billy on his back with Hammond holding his legs out and Hammond's thin hips pumping between in what most know as the missionary position. Once again two shallow and one deep in repeated rhythm. Billy would just lay there, his face turned to the side, counting the faded flowers in the wallpaper of the far wall. The third position—the one Billy thought of as the "he's tired" position—had Hammond on his back and Billy riding his cock. This was the only time variety was permitted, and it had to be Billy who varied the routine if it was to happen at all. Billy could face Hammond or away from him, Hammond didn't care, as long as he could rest and still maintain his erection. In the climax position, rested, Hammond needed to do the driving to the conclusion. Billy was stretched out on his stomach, his eyes cast to the wall on the near side of the bed, once again counting faded flowers, with Hammond crouched over his hips. There was no usual rhythm this time. Hammond was too close to ejaculation at this point to care. This position didn't last for long, as they didn't go into it until Hammond felt he was near to eruption.

Twenty-three minutes. Billy could have almost timed it out to equal length each time—if he had been of a mind too. He had actually done that the third and fourth nights, watching the clock on the mantle at the fireplace because he'd gotten the drift that the routine would be set. But then he lost interest after that. Twenty-three minutes. Seven minutes each to the first three positions and the last one in two or less. It was usually only during this last one, where Billy felt that, at last, Hammond was lost to his need to explode, that Billy managed to explode as well.

50

Billy usually did come sometime in this process. This was still being controlled, if not fucked rough. There was nothing special in Hammond's cock working inside him. But this was still someone controlling him and working out his form of rage on Billy. So, sometime during the process, Billy did work up enough arousal to come himself.

When Hammond had come, he wanted Billy out of the bed immediately, and he just turned over on his side, facing another faded-flower-papered wall and started snoring.

Billy didn't mind. He sensed that he had gone too far in Charleston. Vanilla sex was fine with him for a while. It gave him opportunity to review what he had done and what he really wanted. He knew that what he'd been doing was self-destructive. He just didn't know how to stop. Maybe the way of his father and uncle was best: to work his ass to exhaustion and to keep his sex vanilla and routine. Enough of that and he might lose interest in men. He knew that at some time he would need to take a wife and become as fat and dull as other men of his class. Perhaps taking the thrill and danger away would "cure" Billy of his "illness" just as his father thought it might.

The vanilla routine didn't last for long, though. The day that the levees were all repaired and the fields were flooded for one last time before harvest, it appeared that everything was finally in order on the plantation, with no other immediate chores at hand, toward the late afternoon. The crew moved wearily to a stand of trees in the plantation house's lower garden, just above the river's edge, off to the side of the rice fields, and near where the plantation's wharf ran out into the river. At least Billy was moving wearily, every muscle of his body screaming its objection. Objectionable as it was, though, the work was hardening Billy's body to the point that whereas he had been well formed before, now he was muscled and cut.

"What now?" he asked as he flopped down on the moss under a magnolia tree.

"Tomorrow we begin to check the tools for the harvest to make sure all are in order," said one of the most heavily muscled of the blacks. His skin was a lighter color than most of the others, and he had two names. His first name was Felix, but he was permitted to use Rawley as his surname. Billy had had no trouble understanding why that was. He was a family by-blow by one of the female slaves. Probably a half brother to Charles himself—young enough to be Charles's too, for that matter. Whatever he was, he was often the one who spoke for the group. Spear made the decisions, but Felix voiced what those decisions were.

"But today, now," Felix continued. "We fuck."

"What?" Billy asked, in confusion.

"We fuck you. Spear wants to fuck you. He wants to show a Rawley he is not afraid of them."

"I'm not really a Rawley," Billy objected, but he looked up from where he was sprawled. Spear was standing over him. He was naked and holding a half-hard cock out.

"Make love to it, and then we fuck." It was the most words Billy had yet to hear Spear string together, and his accent was so thick, Billy probably could not have understood what he was saying if it wasn't obvious what he wanted from the belligerent and aggressive stance he was taking. It was almost as if he wanted Billy to try to refuse to suck his cock so that Spear could beat the shit out of him—and then still make him suck the cock.

But Billy complied—gladly. When Spear was pleased with his work, he grunted to Felix, who was naked now as well. In response to Spear's command, Felix lifted Billy up to his feet from behind, laced his arms under Billy's armpits and clamped his fists together at the nape of Billy's neck, immobilizing the young man. Spear moved in close; he lifted and parted Billy's legs and slowing worked his cock into Billy's channel to much moaning and sighing from Billy.

This was far better than Hammond. Billy loved having the black cock inside him. And he loved having Felix hold him captive for the assault.

Fully encased, Spear held there. Billy wrapped his legs around Spear's waist and hooked his ankles above the black slave's bulbous buttocks. His hands free now, Spear touched Billy's chest, tracing the remnants of the whip and cigarette burn scars from Billy's encounters with the Reverend Andrew Apsley, which were fading but were still evident. Billy was being lulled, wondering if this was all that would happen.

But then Spear started to pump him. Hard and deep. And to punch his chest and twist his nipples. Billy opened his mouth to scream, but one of the other slaves was there with a strip of material to gag him. Billy's eyes were wide and watering. But they were alight with fire. He screamed silently again as Felix started to enter his channel with his cock from the rear, pushing in above Spear's now-dormant, but full implanted tool. In their brutal double-penetration fuck, Felix fucked for a while and then rested as Spear resumed the rhythm of the fuck. Billy shot off again and again up Spear's belly until, with much vocalization, Spear and Felix managed to ejaculate nearly simultaneously.

Billy had been silenced, but Felix and Spear hadn't. An underseer heard and then saw the commotion. He went for Hammond, who arrived and watched in hiding from behind some bushes, in time for the climax.

The slaves let Billy slide off their cocks down to the ground. Hammond was taken by surprise, though, when Billy unsteadily rose up on his knees, hugged Spear's legs, and took the slave's cock in his mouth and cleaned it. The overseer realized then that Billy had enjoyed the double fucking by darkies. He turned away in disgust.

Spear raised a foot, planted it in the center of Billy's chest, and pushed Billy to the ground on his back, holding Billy pinned to the ground with his bare foot. He and Felix turned toward the other men of the crew, with Spear giving an invitation to anyone else who wanted to have their turn with Billy. Enough did to occupy the crew until dark. Even Spear showed amazement when Billy opened his legs to the first man who knelt over him and guided the man's cock inside him with his hands.

When Billy struggled to the overseer's house, Hammond came out on the front porch; cursed Billy, telling him he'd have no part of an ass that had been taken by a darky; and told him he could go to the single-men's hut on slave row. Billy did so gladly and was to enjoy his nights better from then on than he had in the overseer's house. Billy could not lie to himself. No he could not prefer the vanilla sex offered by Hammond over the exciting, masterful punishment he received from others, including ebony studs. Being free didn't make your cocking superior.

Out of curiosity, Billy crept up to a window of the overseer's house one night at a particular hour, just to see how much of a man of routine Hammond was. Sure enough, he was going through all four stages of his sex need with one of the younger, more effeminate male house slaves. And Billy could see that the young black man was laying there, counting the faded flowers on the wallpaper just as he'd done.

On the fourth night in the slave men's hut Billy felt the heaviness of Spear's body lower itself on him on his mattress of feathers and corn cobs on the dirt floor, Billy turned his body within Spear's embrace; opened his legs to the giant, already in full erection; and rolled up his pelvis.

"You are so good," Spear murmured. "No more hate fuck. Tonight we make love."

"No, please, Spear. Take me hard again. Keep that hate in your eyes. Remember that I am of the Rawleys. That it was white men like me who brought you here and enslaved you. And I would have done it myself given the chance."

Spear growled his remembrance, rose up on his knees and backhanded Billy across the cheek, snapping Billy's head to the side, putting him into a daze. Billy snapped out of the daze almost immediately, however, as Spear grabbed for his balls and, squeezing them, lifted Billy's pelvis off the surface of the mattress. Billy screamed in pain and glorious anticipation as Spear thrust his cock hard and deep inside Billy's channel, still gripping Billy's balls hard. Eye's watering, gasping for breath, Billy reached down to grip the buttocks of the man assaulting him, and cried out, "Yes, yes. Punish me. Fuck me hard!" The glorious pain of being taken hard and deep and rough in the passion of rage was sending Billy to heaven.

Barely a week later and full of spite and hurt pride, Hammond contacted Charles Rawley in Charleston and told him his nephew was conducting lewd practices with the male slaves.

This was the last straw for the Charleston branch of the family. The last time Billy saw Charles Rawley was on Brown's Wharf as Billy was being put aboard the *Elizabeth*, one of Rawley's merchant vessels, named after his daughter who had sought to seduce Billy herself, and the same vessel that had brought Billy to Charleston from Boston. Billy was being sent as a sailor on the vessel in its journey to deliver a cargo of polished South Carolina rice to Alexandria, Egypt.

Billy tried his best to resist conveying to his long-suffering uncle that this was exactly what he had wanted all along—to be sailing before the mast.

Chapter Three:

On the Atlantic, off the Azores, 1803

Uncle Charles proved to be as dense about identifying men who wanted men in choosing a vessel captain to entrust with his recalcitrant nephew, not to mention one of his precious merchant ships, as he had been about Billy's behavior—and, more pointedly about the Reverend Andrew Apsley he fawned over. Billy's uncle never did seem to latch on to what the good clergymen had done to him for months. Billy had shown his uncle the healing stripes on his body, claiming out of spite, that Hammond had done them rather than Apsley. And all Rawley had said was, "Good, you deserve that and more."

In the event, from what his uncle was ranting to him about the circumstance, Billy gathered that Charles Rawley was more upset about the lost opportunity of linking his family to that of another wealthy planter through the marriage of Billy than he was that Billy preferred rough-fucking men.

Billy could tell that the captain of the company vessel that he was to sail on to the Mediterranean, a different man from the one who had captained the ship on the Boston-to-Charleston run the previous year, was as queer as could be just from the way he watched the young man board his ship. And queer in a way that Billy couldn't quite place. In all the men Billy had been involved with, none acted quite like this one did. Of course he had heard of Billy's proclivities. By the way he leaned way over the rail and licked his lips and flashed his eyes—

fluttered his eyelashes—as Billy walked up the gangway and into his clutches for the long voyage across the ocean, the younger man knew what he was in for. All he could think of was the hope that the captain was a cruel lover, although the almost coquettish way the captain looked at him seemed to put that possibility into question.

Billy didn't know all that he would be in for, however.

It was not the sexual opportunities and burdens that Billy first thought of in the experience of going to sea before the mast, which is where Rawley told the captain to put him—with the other common sailors—as a punishment that the man would have no appreciation that Billy would enjoy. The experience of learning the ropes and watches as a three-master barque sailor was one of the best of Billy's life. He took to the work immediately. It was nowhere near as hard as growing rice, and he'd only been in on one weeding and the harvesting of that. Billy wasn't sure he'd claim that he could have survived the complete growing season, and he could well understand that the only ones who would survive those conditions were slaves who had little other choice. Of course, he was as much a slave to other men as Spear and his companions were.

The chores on board were varied, however, and they left Billy muscle tired beyond exhaustion for the first two weeks of the voyage. He would come to his hammock in the forecastle totally spent but also totally satisfied with what he had learned and experienced that day—and how free he felt climbing the rigging, watching the unending sea open to the plowing of the ship, and feeling the breeze cool his body. Although it was September, the ship was taking a southern route, and the sailors wore next to nothing to keep as cool as possible.

Billy was in good shape from the hard work he'd done on the rice plantation, but most of the other men were even more heavily muscled than he was. Most of them were larger than he was too, even though some were gaunt from age and the hard demands of a sailor's life. Billy was often still taken for a boy rather than a young man of nearly nineteen years. In terms of sexual desire, though, being taken for a boy was no protection from men such as these—it was rather the opposite.

They were a rough and ugly lot, on the whole, and other than a couple of cabin boys, Billy stood out as the most desirable morsel for any sniffing about for that. Having adapted to versatility by the nature of their life of long spans of time without access to women, something like Billy was exactly what the sailors were looking for. In port, they fucked women mostly; on ship they were forced to fuck other men exclusively.

They fucked because they were compelled to—there were few other pleasures available to them on the sea. The pickings usually were so marginally acceptable that any young, good-looking man who came their way did not, under any circumstances, remain a virgin to the cock for long—whether or not he liked it, and, interesting enough, men on the high seas relegated to the "receiver" role in man-on-man sex tended to adapt to it. As a "receiver" aged and became hardened as a sailor, he could turn into topping others, as he liked. Until then, however, his ass was claimed by any man—or combination of men—who could physically master him. If he couldn't adapt, he tended to be lost at sea.

During the first week, Billy, berthed in the forecastle with the common sailors, was fucked at least twice every night after his second night. The second night aboard, he was fucked continuously through the night and was unable to work the next day. After that, the first mate proclaimed that Billy was off limits for more than three visits a night and that he was to be accorded at least four hours straight for sleep. "He is aboard to work in the rigging, not on his back," the first mate said. "Any day the lad is unable to turn out for his duty is the day his jobs are added to the duties of them who fucked him the previous night." That effectively put Billy's ass on a less-taxing schedule, and the other men made up a primitive chart on whose turn it would be with him on a given night.

It remained, however, that Billy was the most desirable—and smallest of stature—piece in the forecastle, so first mate, or no, as long as he was berthed there, he would be fucked nightly. The first mate understood this and only put limits on the activity; he made no attempt to stop it. And Billy, who reveled in the need to be "punished" like this, made no complaint. Most of the men were ugly, certainly, but they also were rough, which Billy liked, and in the dark, one cock is pretty much like any other.

The young apprentice sailor wasn't assaulted the first night. He worked little that day because it required more experienced hands than his to put the ship to sea, and this was not time to be giving lessons. That night, with the sailors having worked especially hard themselves that day, Billy was able to cajole his way free of attention and to remain awake and vigilant through much of the night. After the first full day of working on deck and in the rigging, though, he was able to do nothing but crawl into his hammock and drift off into a dead sleep. The first brave man, one of the dominating forces in the forecastle, just climbed into the hammock with Billy, split his legs, and sent the hammock to rocking even more than the moving ship did by plowing his hole. Billy just lay there, exhausted, as the sailor knew he would be, his arms dangling over the side of the hammock, and languidly watching the other sailors take notice and begin to circle around them like sharks.

Although this was at sea rather than on land, other than in the relative size of the cocks and vigor of the fuck, this was little different from what Billy had recently been experiencing in the men's slave hut at the plantation. He was long past objecting to opening his legs and receiving any man's cock.

When the sailor was finished, he lifted Billy out of the hammock and gave him up into the arms of two sailors who were so anxious to get at him that they were willing to share his channel. Billy did none of the screaming of violation that the sailors expected of such a double assault, but just lay, arms dangling and legs wrapped around the thighs of the man facing him, his head resting in the hollow of the shoulder of the sailor behind. He ejaculated during the fucking, so the sailors decided he was having a pleasant enough time—which he was other than, for a change, desiring sleep more than rough sex.

After that, it was a night of just passing Billy from one erect cock to the other. So randy did the sailors become that one of them went out on deck and intercepted one of the cabin boys, barely younger than Billy and not any larger, and brought him into the forecastle to share around as well. In the morning the cabin boy was laying on his back, his knees wagging open because he couldn't close them, and moaning softly to himself, which raised the occasion of the visit by the first mate to parcel out his daily duties across the forecastle—except to Billy—and the warning of what would happen if Billy couldn't appear to take up his position in the rigging on the next day.

Even though Billy was in a haze throughout the experience—if not particularly upset by it, as it was not the first such group taking he had been the object of in the last month, the black slaves on the plantation capable of doing it with bigger and longer cocks and more vigorously and with greater stamina. He was able to notice that one sailor, a black man of musculature, if not height, to equal any of the slaves at Rawley Place, save Spear himself, was sitting off in the shadows. He was watching, but he wasn't participating. Billy assumed that he was a rare sailor whose cock wouldn't seek any port. He obviously was the most respected—or feared, or both—man in the forecastle, however, as indicated by the deference everyone gave him and the wide path they accorded him as they moved about. Billy was to be told later that he was Black Ned, a Nubian from the deserts of northern Africa. That he knew all there was to know about sailing the Atlantic and the Mediterranean, and that he took whatever he wanted, whenever he wanted to take it.

Indeed, belying Billy's first impression, after the first mate departed the forecastle, Black Ned came down from his perch on a top bunk at the rear of the forecastle, came over and toed the inert body of the cabin boy, being rewarded with a low moan. He thereupon scooped the cabin boy's body up from the deck and carried him back to the bunk. He laid him down on the edge of the bottom bunk, wishboned the lad's legs, unbuttoned his own fly, and began fucking the cabin boy with long, hard strokes that had the young man whimpering, writhing anew, and weakly begging for mercy.

Some would have seen that as a delayed building of desire. But Billy recognized it for the challenge it was. Black Ned didn't desire the cabin boy's well-used ass. He was making a statement of defiance of the first mate's dictum.

The act of defiance didn't stop there. Although Billy didn't have to work that day, he did have to piss. After the sun had been up a couple of hours, need forced Billy to stumble out onto the deck. He lurched to the side of the ship, unbuttoned his cut-off trousers, and started pissing a great arc into the sea. He felt a man covering him close from behind, and looked down to see a brown hand encase his cock, He was still pissing when the hand started to jerk him off. The man's other hand was pushing his trousers down around his knees. Two fingers and then three were invading his channel.

The voice at his ear was deep and menacing. "You are going to come for me while I get this whole fist up in you and then I'm going to fuck you as a man should be fucked."

Billy moaned, knowing that it was Black Ned at his back. This was happening out on deck. The men around them stopped their work to watch. Billy could even see that the first mate, standing at watch on the upper deck, could see what Black Ned was doing. He called out nothing to Black Ned, however. All that he did was to yell at the other men to see to their work. Those that were able saw to what Black Ned was doing with Billy in addition to seeing to their work.

The sailor apprentice was moaning and his eyes were watering as Black Ned stroked his cock and stuffed another finger inside him. Billy's feet were nearly lifted off the deck—he was standing on his tiptoes—and he ejaculated as he felt the knuckles of Black Ned's hand inside his rim.

"You want this. You love this," Black Ned muttered.

"Yes. Don't stop. But fuck me now. The cock; give me the cock," Billy begged. He was being fucked, but it was with Black Ned's half-buried fist.

"From now on, I am first," Black Ned growled.

"Yes," Billy acceded.

"And you come to me."

"Yes. Oh god, oh god. Your cock. Give me the cock," Billy cried out.

He had been gripping roping overhead to keep his balance until that point, but Black Ned slapped his hands off the ropes, and Billy's body pitched forward, his eyes now looking at the churning wake of the waves that the ship was slicing through. Only Black Ned's strong grip on Billy's waist kept him from falling into the sea.

That's when Black Ned showed Billy that he had the thickest cock on the ship.

On ensuing nights, Billy climbed up to Black Ned's upper bunk at the back of the forecastle first and rode the Nubian's cock before he came down to find out what other sailors' names had come up on the evening's chart. Billy had found the satisfying Alpha dog that he had been searching for on the ship.

However, after two weeks, the first mate put an immediate stop to Billy's nightly takings, Billy having become wildly popular by insisting that each man do his worst with him, simply by letting the men know that Billy was the nephew of the ship's owner, that his hard work only extended to his job as an apprentice sailor, and that he would be sleeping with the officers from henceforth.

Sleeping with the officers, of course, meant even more demanding sex from more educated and sophisticated men with more positions and imaginative ways to tax a bottom.

The third week, as the ship was approaching the Azores, the captain at last revealed his own desire. Billy didn't know why he had held off so long, but perhaps it had to do with the perverse nature of his fetish and with the possibility that Billy would report it to his uncle. Apparently, however, the officers had become so open and detailed in their discussions and boasts of what Billy would allow them to do to him and how he would beg for even rougher sex—and how good a lay Billy was—that the captain couldn't resist.

When Billy entered the cabin, he did a double take, as he hadn't realized that there were any women aboard. But there, sitting on a bench seat below the fantail window in the captain's cabin was the visage of a woman, dressed in formal costume.

It was only as Billy was beckoned closer that he discovered it was the captain, dressed as a woman—and quite expertly made up and coiffured as a woman. Even his chest was pushed up and sheathed to give the impression of breasts.

Billy faltered.

"Do not be afraid, Billy," the captain whispered in a voice set falsely high. "I do have a cock, and I will use it with you. And, trust me, I know how to use it. Come, sit beside me."

Billy looked around, hoping there was someone else present he could reason with or seek explanation from. But he had been delivered here by an officer of the ship, and he very much suspected the officer was standing just on the other side of the door. Billy had heard a lock click from the other side of the door when he had entered and it closed behind him.

"Captain, sir . . ." Billy started to say, but then he realized there was nothing he could say. They were out on the Atlantic. This man was god and king of his vessel out here. And Billy was neither naïve nor a virgin.

"Come, please, sit beside me. I don't bite—unless, of course, during our lovemaking you would wish me to. You do know that you are here to be fucked, I assume. I understand there is no trouble in getting you to open your legs. Have you never been fucked by a man dressed as a woman before?"

"No . . . sir, I haven't."

"So, you don't know whether you would be aroused by it or not, do you?"

"No, sir, I don't."

"All you need to do is to treat me like a woman. I know that that might be distasteful to you, but all of the time you do so, you can remember that I have a cock, and that it will please you and make you come."

Billy sat down on the bench beside the "woman," who reached out and caressed his face lightly with the fingers of "her" hand. The captain leaned into Billy and they kissed, which felt no different to Billy than the kiss of any other man save for the taste of the lip rouge.

When the "woman" pulled away from Billy, "she" leaned back in the bench, jutted "her" chest out, and commanded, "Free my breasts and make love to them."

Billy slowly unlaced the "woman's" bodice. The captain wasn't young and wasn't in the best of shape, so the breasts actually were slightly pendulous. The nipples were prominent and had been rouged. The "woman" cupped the back of Billy's head and brought his lips to a nipple. As instructed, he sucked and teethed it and then moved to the other one and back, as the captain sighed and moaned.

Billy's cut-off sailor's trousers were being unbuttoned, and the captain extracted and stroked his cock.

"Put your hand up under my skirt and feel what I have for you."

The captain was naked under the skirt, His cock was erect and thick and his balls were gargantuan.

"I assure you I can fuck with the best," the captain murmured. "I can punish."

The key word had been spoken, the images of being taken roughly had emerged, and Billy's own cock began to harden.

"Sit on it now."

His trousers off, making Billy naked, the front of the captain's skirt was raised, and Billy sat in his lap, facing him, and slid his channel on the cock.

"Crouch on the bench on your heels and keep yourself raised off me. I'll do the fucking."

Billy did so and arched his back away from the captain, and now it was the captain kissing, sucking, and chewing on Billy's nipples as he fucked up into his channel in long, deep thrusts.

Billy was feeling the power of the captain's driving cock when all hell broke loose on the deck above them. It was clear that the ship was being boarded in the twilight, and, from the sound of it, it seemed equally clear that the ship's men had been utterly surprised and outnumbered and outclassed.

Billy, rose quickly off the captain's cock. The captain, nearly lost in arousal, was slower to respond. Billy had no time to do more than grab up a short sword from a nearby table and turn to the door, when that same door burst open and Black Ned spun into the room. Billy could see the first mate beyond him, laying lifeless in the corridor outside the door. The Nubian was being closely engaged in hand-to-hand sword combat by a swarthy pirate. Spinning in behind Black Ned's assailant was one for Billy too, a muscle-bound Scandinavian giant twice the size of Black Ned's opponent, stripped to the waist and covered in tattoos. A black giant of a man tried to swarm in behind him but was stopped in the doorway because the cabin was hardly big enough to hold the combatants and petrified "lady" already in attendance and still trying to recover from the indignity of his ship being attacked while he was in costume.

Black Ned ran his opponent through the gut with his sword, leaving no doubt that the man had been dispatched. At the same time, Billy's sword tip found a soft spot near the abdomen of the Scandinavian. As both men fell, the black giant found room to enter and pierced Black Ned's side with his sword. Billy pulled his own sword out of the Scandinavian and sliced at the black giant's sword arm just as he was preparing to finish Black Ned. This assailant turned to Billy with a look of surprise and malevolence in his eyes, and Billy was about to run him through when the doorway was filled with yet another figure.

The others now were joined by the apparent pirate crew leader, a magnificent figure of a man, dressed fancier and with more ruffles than his compatriots, and honored with the benefit of two flintlock pistols rather than cutlery. Billy heard a loud noise and saw a puff of smoke enveloping the visage of this late-arriving figure, and all went black.

When Billy became half conscious again, his first sensation was of a burning sensation in his scalp above his ear, where the ball had grazed his head and laid him out cold. His next memory was of the screaming from the adjacent cabin of the "wench" who had been seducing Billy before the unpleasantness began. Clearly someone else was interested that the ship was transporting a woman. The moment didn't last long. Whoever was trying to assault the female version of the captain had discovered the truth, and the raging objection and the scream and gurgle from the captain told Billy that that little unusual vignette had come to a close and that his uncle's employ was now minus one ship's captain.

Billy's next memory was the most painful of all. His hands were tied off with rope above his head around a leg of the captain's desk in the center of the cabin, and Billy was stretched out on the desk, belly to wood. He felt a familiar pressure in his intestines and soon became aware that the fancy pirate chief had his cock up his ass and was churning away inside him.

He and his men had caught Billy at a distinct disadvantage in total nakedness, and the pirate chief must have taken an instant liking to what he saw, obviously preferring Billy to the "woman" other members of his crew had so briefly and unsatisfactorily been playing with in the adjacent cabin. Now he was penetrating Billy deeply, and the danger of it all was having Billy crying out with passion, the pirate reasonably assuming it was with objection, but Billy knowing it was from the adrenalin of the roughness and forced nature of it. The pirate pulled Billy's head back toward him with a grip on the hair Billy had tied off in a tail, arching his back. With his other hand, the assailant brutally turned Billy's head to him and possessed his mouth with a churning and searching tongue until Billy was near unto gagging. He continued to pump away madly at Billy's ass, somewhat surprised that Billy was punching back, seeking a rhythm, wanting the cock. At length, the pirate chief let loose of Billy's head, moved his hands down to the young sailor's pecs on either side, and dug long fingernails into the aureoles surrounding the nipples that the ship's captain had so recently chewed raw. Billy screamed out with pain-pleasure.

To try to control the pain from the brutal taking, Billy looked into the corner of the cabin, where the black giant, a rough bandage around his sliced arm the only clothes he now was wearing, was force-feeding a long and hard, but not terribly thick cock into Black Ned's mouth. Black Ned was on his knees, his chest was covered in blood from his own wound, and the black giant was holding a knife under his chin to encourage Black Ned to give him good suck.

Billy was being pushed up on the table top by the strength of the pirate's ramming cock, and he screamed and writhed back and forth, successfully causing the pirate chief's long and thick cock to dislodge from his ass, but the struggling served Billy not. The pirate chief turned him onto his back on the table and rendered him unconscious again with two heavy fist blows to the face. When Billy regained consciousness, the pirate chief was fucking him in the ass again, but this time Billy was below him on his back and the pirate was wish-boning his legs out and up from his body. When the pirate saw that Billy was conscious, he pushed his legs down along his body, Billy's toes pointing toward his head, and brought his own torso down on top of Billy's and attacked his nipples and mouth with his teeth. The pirate was looking into Billy's eyes and grinning a silly grin and clearly enjoying the yelp Billy gave with every deep thrust he made with his cock.

"Oh god, yes," Billy murmured. "Fuck me. Punish me." But such was the noise from the fighting on deck that the pirate chief didn't hear.

The pirate chief's fist went to the wound in Billy head and the young sailor saw fireworks, felt maddening pain, and fainted once more.

This time when Billy awoke, he was out on the open deck, strung up with rope around both wrists, which were tied off on the rigging of a mast overhead. Black Ned was similarly tied off, facing Billy, not more than twenty feet away. The pirate chief stood between them, at a right angle to the two captives, his legs splayed out in a wide stance, a satisfied smirk on his face, and his arms crossed on his chest, a flintlock in each hand. He was stripped to the waist, showing a magnificent barrel chest, and his horse-hung cock still dangled from his open codpiece. Billy wondered that all of that had been stuffed up him, but the searing pain in his ass canal, despite the almost constant use it had been getting, left Billy little doubt that it had been.

Billy watched in horror and fascination as the black giant fucked the smaller Nubian, Black Ned, from behind with his long, long cock. With what Billy had seen the black giant packing, he thought that surely the cock was making its way into Ned's stomach. Black Ned wasn't accustomed to being the one who was fucked. The black giant was bent at the knees and was swinging Black Ned's butt back onto his battering ram of a cock with beefy hands lodged under the other man's thighs. Black Ned obviously wasn't enjoying this treatment nearly as much as the black giant was.

Seeing that Billy was awake again, the pirate chief came around behind him and entered his ass again with his cock, sliding in to the hilt and sending ripples of pain—and, yes, of pleasure too—around Billy's ass walls. Two of his men held Billy's legs out while the pirate chief plowed him yet again. The pirate chief wrapped his arms around Billy, buried his lips and teeth into the side of his neck, and his hands, now bereft of his flintlocks, locked onto Billy's manhood. The young sailor was greatly frightened that his cock hardened up for him, not wanting the pirates to know that he loved it rough, but there was nothing he could do to hide his arousal. He spilled his seed on the rough planks of the vessel's deck.

The pirate laughed, taking this as an indication that the handsome, young sailor that he couldn't keep his hands off, was inexperienced to the cocks of men.

While this was going on, Billy saw a bundle of petticoats, which he recognized as the unfortunately garbed merchant vessel's captain, being carried out of the officer's cabin area and thrown over the side of the ship. The bodies of other dispatched sailors from the *Elizabeth* were being similarly disposed of.

The black giant grew bored with his fucking of Black Ned and pulled away from him. The pirate chief suddenly tensed and bathed Billy's insides with his cum. He then pulled out of him as well and returned to his stance between the two trussed-up captives. Waving a reacquired flintlock in Black Ned's direction, the pirate chief declared that Black Ned had killed one of his best men. "What then," he asked his assembled men, "should we do with him?" The word "death" rang around the deck.

"How about death by belaying pin?" the pirate chief asked in a ringing voice, and boisterous assents were given all around. At a signal, one of the other pirates brought out a belaying pin that was well over a foot long and several inches thick, and disappeared behind Black Ned. Black Ned's head lifted in a scream and howl, gurgling to silence.

After Black Ned had been dispatched, the pirate chief's flintlock then turned to Billy, and he told the two men Billy had wounded and who now were naked except for the dressings on their wounds that they could have at the young sailor together if they liked in compensation for their wounds. They obviously liked, because the Scandinavian approached Billy from the rear, with his long, thick manhood at attention, and the black giant, with his longer but thinner cock, also at attention, approached Billy from the front, other ruffians lifted and spread Billy's legs wide apart, and the two assailants Billy had supposedly wronged both entered his ass with their ram rods and began fluttering their hands all over his body and each other. The cocks of the two pumped Billy in counter piston action until both pirates had come, almost simultaneously.

Once again, Billy's passionate cries of satisfaction were misinterpreted as screams of terror and tearing asunder of his insides. Billy's looks were deceiving. His channel had been prepared for this. Still, Billy was frightened—frightened to the heights of arousal. He ejaculated again to the amazed laughter of the gathered pirates, knowing in his heart that he was about to die, but also knowing he was going at the height of passion and gratification.

Billy thought the ordeal was about over, even if it was to climax in death, but when the two were finished with him and had pulled their dicks out of him with a sucking sound, the pirate chief asked his crew what should be done with the handsome young sailor, the greatest prize they had found on the ship. Billy once more heard the sickening word "death" being proclaimed to the winds. The pirate chief looked around the deck, obviously searching for something, and then all eyes, including Billy's, went to the railing around the bridge over the officer's cabins. Each separate section of the railing was topped off by a newel post. Each post was topped with a round, wooden ball of some four inches in diameter that was commonly used to contain tie offs of ropes from the rigging.

"Death by post ball," the pirate chief declared in a ringing voice, and all voices but Billy's agreed with a great deal of mirth. Billy had no illusion how they planned to use one of those four-inch post balls, and he began to jabber and sob. Black Ned's fist had just about been the death of him, but it had not been quite as large, had not fully penetrated him, and had been flexible. Black Ned himself had just died from having a thinner wooden staff thrust up inside him.

"Or perhaps you would prefer this," the pirate chief announced with a laugh. He then walked back over to Billy and slid the cold barrel of one of his flintlocks up Billy's ass. With a sickening sensation, Billy heard him pull the trigger, which was followed by a dull click. The pirate's crew roared with laughter at this excellent joke. Billy's knees gave way and he almost fainted. Still, he felt himself going hard again.

The black giant and the Scandinavian were untying Billy's ropes from the rigging and starting to manhandle him up the stairs to the bridge, where all could better see the entertainment, when there were new shouts heard at the far side of the ship, and all turned to see yet more sailors, armed to the teeth, coming over the sides.

Looking down into the murky nighttime water, Billy saw that there were other small, open boats on this side of the merchant vessel. Reinforcements were preparing to come up this side as well, he thought.

In the turmoil, the men who had been manhandling him turned to the new danger. Only now did Billy realize that these were not pirate reinforcement, but were competition. He climbed up on the rail and dove into the water, his presence now completely ignored by the pirate chief and crew who had raped him and killed his companions. They had themselves been caught by surprise and were now fighting for their own lives.

The water was cold, and Billy was weak from the recent assaults on his body, but he managed to dogpaddle to one of the open boats, where strong arms pulled him up into the boat.

There was only one sailor in the boat. He must have let off his comrades on the other side of the merchant vessel and been sent around on this side for safety and to pick off any of the pirates who had tried to escape this way, Billy thought. He was even bigger and more heavily muscled than the Scandinavian pirate had been. And he was stripped to the waist; was covered in tattoos, and obviously was ready for action. His eyes were locked on Billy's body, and his mouth was hanging open in surprise.

With a sigh, Billy turned over on his back in the shell of the row boat, slung his legs over the sides, rolled up his pelvis, and resigned himself to another fucking.

Chapter Four:

Saved and Escorted to the Azores: 1803

Billy had not been pirated again. Instead a somewhat confused American naval man from the USS *Philadelphia* rowed him directly back to his own ship, where he was handed a pair of trousers, rowed back to the *Elizabeth*, and kept under guard and separated from anyone else while the naval officers of the *Philadelphia*, under the command of William Bainbridge, worked to sort out who was merchant sailor and who was pirate.

In the chaos that still reigned, the pirate ship, which had been standing off the *Elizabeth* a good distance, managed to slip over the horizon, abandoning its captain and coconspirators.

Luckily, the pirates hadn't had time to take full control of the *Elizabeth* and to search every nook and cranny of the ship. Enough officers of the merchant vessel and other crew members had survived to identify Billy not only as a member of the *Elizabeth*'s crew but as the nephew of the ship's owner as well. This was enough to bring him before Bainbridge, who knew how to curry favor with the American merchant class.

Billy hadn't occupied one of the three passenger cabins on the ship to this point, being relegated to the forecastle initially and then taken into the officer's quarters. Bainbridge assumed one of the passenger cabins was where he belonged, however, as he was the nephew of the owner, and Billy didn't object to being assigned a passenger cabin. Bainbridge suggested that Billy might want to go to his cabin on the *Elizabeth* while they dealt with the pirates who survived. He assumed that the hangings would be too traumatizing for a young man who obviously had already experienced the unspeakable—an unspeakable that Bainbridge would ignore happened—and who was of the family of the ship's owner. No one, including Billy, corrected his impression. It would have been just too confusing for him to understand that Billy was sailing as an apprentice sailor as punishment for enjoying rough sex—with men. Which is precisely what the pirate captain had been giving him when Bainbridge's forces arrived.

The young man went meekly to a passenger cabin, however, and tried to filter out the sounds of summary trial and execution coming from the deck above. The whole experience had, in fact, been traumatizing for him beyond his fetish for the danger and his perceived love for pirates. His intellectualization both of what pirates did and how they were dealt with when captured had been far more romanticized than the reality that had hit him between the eyes. The fucking by the pirate chief hadn't been bad at all, and even the teasing of his death had exhilarated Billy and lifted him to the heights of hardness. But the brutal killing of Black Ned before his eyes had shaken him to the core—as had the evidence of his own planned demise.

After dispensing with the pirates, Bainbridge augmented the survivors of the *Elizabeth* with naval sailors from the *Philadelphia*, putting one of his own senior officers in charge, and declared that the *Philadelphia* would escort the *Elizabeth* to the Azores, a three-day sail away, where Charles Rawley eventually could be reached to sort out what to do with his interrupted rice delivery and depleted ship's crew. Bainbridge consulted with Billy on these matters as if he represented the owner, and Billy wagged his head in feigned interest as if he did.

Once more on deck, Billy offered to help set the sails of the *Elizabeth*, which the new commanding officer, Lt. Edward Foster, considered quite a magnanimous offer.

"I know a bit about working in the rigging," Billy answered. "You saved our ship and some of the crew, and have not just abandoned us and gone your way, so I will be happy to lend a hand to the Azores."

"Capital," Foster answered, impressed, and clearly taken with the handsome young ship owner's kin. "I pray that you will not overtax yourself, however. And do not tarry at it for long. I hope to see you at the officer's table for supper tonight."

Billy answered that he'd be pleased to be there, and then, alongside the surviving sailors of the *Elizabeth* and the augmenting naval sailors from the *Philadelphia*, he jumped up into the rigging as nearly as nimble a monkey as any of the other seasoned sailors.

Lieutenant Foster watched him scramble overhead with admiration—and with the glimmer of another interest altogether.

Working alongside the naval sailors was invigorating for Billy. They weren't a bit like the sailors of a merchantmen. They were all young and in top physical condition—and they were more intelligent and outgoing than the sailors Billy had become used to. He made friends quickly.

There were the naval sailors Clem, Jocko, Slice, and Big Luke, two first voyagers and two in their second year before the mast, but all young and fit and boisterous and easy to joke with. And Billy became friends with two Marines as well, Hal and Dirk. The Marines on board—the contingent having been split between the *Philadelphia* and the *Elizabeth*—were not like the sailors. They knew little of sailing and had no duties in the rigging. The unit was a new one for the Navy, necessitated by the piracy they were combating. The Marines were essentially hand-to-hand combat soldiers being included on ships of the line as assault soldiers as needed upon boarding other vessels. These men were particularly fit, heavy of muscle, and nimble. They spent most of their days in combat training on the deck. Although Hal and Dirk were nearly inseparable, they were quite unlike, Hal being blond and smooth skinned and Dirk dark and hirsute. In physique, however, they were much of one cut, as were all the Marines—magnificently built. The naval sailors Billy befriended were also handsome and well formed. He marveled—out loud—at how different they were, as a group, from the grizzled merchantman vessel sailors Billy knew.

"That is a requirement for serving in the U.S. Navy," Jocko jokingly responded to Billy when he noted that the sailors on this vessel were quite unlike those on the *Elizabeth*.

"Methinks the main reason is that the naval service itself is so young," Slice added. "The sea will make us ugly and deformed fast enough, I am sure. You yourself would make a good Navy man, I reckon—if, if course, you were not so small of stature and fair looking."

He gave Billy a wink then that told the young man that the naval men probably weren't much off from the ones he'd known on the *Elizabeth* in terms of interests and needs.

Billy broached this subject with the other friend he quickly gained, the cabin boy, Adam, who was even smaller in stature than Billy was, nearly a year younger, willowy of body, and with a pretty face ringed with blond curls and punctuated with watery blue eyes and a sunny smile.

"I hear that naval men are not of the same class as merchant sailors in this way," Adam answered. "Or at least not as much. They rotate between sea duty and duty on land, and I think this keeps their frustration down somewhat."

"And then you have no trouble with the sailors on the *Philadelphia*?" Billy asked. This was a wonder to him if it were true. Such as Adam would be swarmed over on the *Elizabeth*.

Adam blushed. "I hear that you would understand. Otherwise I would not speak of it. I have a lover. Lieutenant Foster. Knowing this, the other men do not bother me . . . much."

"And it is good with Foster?" Billy asked. Billy himself had some interest in that direction. He thought on the pretty, small cabin boy with the nearly six-and-a-half-foot, broad-shouldered ship's officer, and it made him go hard.

Adam was looking dreamy eyed now. "Yes, he has a way with the strap that makes me just . . ."

The lad didn't complete the sentence. Having been put to the strap on more than one occasion himself and succumbing to its dark pleasures in his need for punishment in sex, Billy had experience in this himself. His thoughts went back to the right reverend Apsley in Charleston. But in a visual inspection of Adam's body, stripped to the waist as were all of the naval

74

sailors—but not the Marines—while they were working in the rigging, Billy could find no evidence of the strap.

He shrank from the image now, but there was a time when he would have spilled his seed just imagining a tall, strong, handsome man like Lieutenant Foster working his body with a whip as the man's cock got hard as a rock for the fucking.

At dinner, Foster treated Billy like the owner of the ship—and so, then, did all of the other officers, including the surviving ones from the *Elizabeth*, who, no doubt, were hoping that Billy would not reveal how they had passed him around from berth to berth during the previous week. For his part, Billy, revealed nothing of the position or treatment he'd received previous to the pirate attack. Nor did he say anything about the nature of how he had fared during the pirate attack. The pirates had been grilled on their behavior before they were hanged, however, and it was not a great secret what the pirate chief had done with Billy. This was known not just in the officers' quarters but among all of the sailors, merchantmen and naval sailors alike, as word of the licentious travels fast on a sailing vessel, especially when most of the sailors either already knew what Billy could and would do for them or hoped that he would do for them before the cruise was completed.

None, of course, referred to it openly, but undoubtedly Billy's proclivities were shared with all by his former shipmates.

While they ate, Billy watched Foster's eyes follow Adam around the cabin, as the lad helped with the serving, and he could tell that Adam had not lied about their liaison. He trembled a bit, too, when he saw that Foster gave him a similar interest of the eye.

In their dinner discussion, Foster told Billy why the *Philadelphia* had been in the eastern Atlantic. He noted that for decades, the Barbary Coast countries—those in northern Africa on the Mediterranean Sea, Tripoli, Tunis, Algiers, and Morocco, had sanctioned official piracy on the merchant ships of all of the European and New World countries that were trading in and across the Mediterranean. The Arab states, principally Tripoli and Algiers, demanded tribute for not attacking the shipping, and both the European nations and the new American nation had paid it. There still were pirate attacks, but they were kept at the level of functioning as a reminder of what could happen if the tribute wasn't paid.

The Pasha of Tripoli, Yussif Karamanli, who had recently deposed his elder brother, Hamet, had increased the demands. The new American president, Thomas Jefferson, who had unsuccessfully opposed the paying of the tribute as early as 1784 when he was seconded to Benjamin Franklin as U.S. envoy to France, balked at the new demands. Now that he was president, he declared, in fact, that the United States would no longer pay any tribute, and he was sending a naval force into the Mediterranean to blockade Tripoli's ports and to suppress Barbary Coast piracy. The frigate, the USS *Philadelphia*, was on its way to be a key vessel in this effort. That was why it had come across the pirate attack on the *Elizabeth*, which was flying an American flag and thus had a right to aid from the *Philadelphia*. The two ships would go to the Azores, near the mouth of the Atlantic entrance in the Mediterranean, where the *Elizabeth* would be docked awaiting word of its future from Charleston and the *Philadelphia*'s crew would be reunited to continue its mission in North Africa.

"I thank you for your hospitality," Billy said to Lieutenant Foster at the end of the meal, "but I regret that I will need to decline your offer of after-dinner port, as I am exhausted. I know I'll sleep the sleep of the dead tonight."

"No, it is for me to thank you for the hospitality," Foster countered congenially, "It is your ship and your food and port we are enjoying. And I have thoroughly enjoyed our conversation. I can well understand your need for sleep, and I only hope that it is a very pleasant one."

Billy indeed felt near to collapse as he returned to his cabin. It had been a long and harrowing day. He slipped out of the officer's clothing that had been provided for him for his visit to the captain's table, and fell onto the berth—and immediately into a deep sleep.

In the darkest hour of the night, he only slowly came into the consciousness of a man's body laying fully prone on top of him as he was sprawled on the berth, naked, on his belly.

The man already was deep inside him, slowly stroking, deep, and, in his sleep, Billy had responded as he was accustomed to respond. He was raised slightly on his knees, offering his entrance to a convenient angle for the fuck. He murmured he knew not what, and a deep, somewhat familiar, man's educated voice answered him with endearments on how sweet and desirable he was and how he would be treated right and given every satisfaction.

The man pulled out of him and took Billy's hand and pressed it on the hard cock that had been working inside him, whispering, "This is all for you."

Billy shuddered. The cock was not thick, but it was unusually long. He tried holding his breath as it slowly slid back inside him, but he could not suppress the moan at the feel of the long, deep slide repossessing him.

Billy felt lips at his throat and a tongue in his ear, and he turned his face to one that he could not make out in the darkness and permitted his lips to be possessed. He heard the intake of breath and the sigh when he raised up higher on his knees and opened his stance to allow deeper, more open access to his channel.

This clearly was taken as a signal of acceptance, and, with a groan and grunts, the rhythm and rate of the plowing picked up. It wasn't a rough fuck, but it was a hard, deep fuck, ending in a flood of cum.

Billy had no idea how long his channel was being mined before he woke, but it wasn't long before his lover—Billy couldn't think of this man as an assailant; he was a lover just as the schoolmaster, Sam, had been a lover, or had meant to be—trembled and jerked and held their body's in suspension for a second or more, and then ejaculated in three strong flowings deep inside Billy's channel. Billy moaned his total surrender, as rather than pulling out immediately, the cock made four long slides out and then back in. Billy shuddered and then he too came—not for the last time.

The stranger turned Billy onto his back and lay against his side for several moments, running his hands over Billy's body and murmuring his pleasure and thanks. A hand went to Billy's cock and began to slow pump him, and Billy mewed quietly and turned his face to the stranger's for another, long, lingering kiss. He could see the face enough to discern the fairness of it but not well enough to attach a name to it, although he knew he'd heard the voice recently. Billy too took these moments to glide his hands over the smooth, hard torso muscles of the lover. A hand descended to the man's now, momentarily flaccid, cock, and Billy gasped once again at the length of it, even in repose.

Then lips were working their way down Billy's body, and the man, who Billy had discerned by the movement of his own hands was magnificently cut and muscled reversed himself above Billy. As a wet mouth descended on Billy's cock, Billy raised his own mouth to the stranger's cock, which began to reharden at the touch of Billy's lips.

He had never sucked another man as tenderly as this— or been sucked as lovingly or thoroughly himself. When it was evident Billy was ready to come again, strong hands raised his buttocks up, his cock slid deep into the throat of this dark-of-the-night lover, and he was drained dry of his cum.

"Are you overtaxed?" the man murmured when they were entwined side by side again.

"Never enough. You . . . you are so long," Billy whispered back, although it was clear that he had no strength left.

The man gave a low laugh, "And you are able to sheath it all. I could fuck you forever."

And forever seemed a possibility. The stranger, taller, larger, and stronger than Billy, moved to the edge of the berth and sat there, his feet on the ground. He reached around and gathered Billy to him and sat Billy, facing him, in his lap. Billy was fully pliant, letting the other man manipulate him at will. Billy's legs were moved to where they ran up the man's chest on either side of his head—a head and face that Billy still could not make out in the darkness.

The man was hard again, and pulled Billy's channel onto his cock. Billy's torso hung out over the decking beyond the edge of the berth and his arms and head dangled down in glorious exhaustion. The man was holding him out with broad, strong hands gripping the young man's sides just below his pecs, with the man's thumbs pressing into Billy's nipples.

In long strokes, with the glans of the man's penis almost reaching the surface and then, in a long slide, reaching as far up into Billy's channel as it could, the man started to pull Billy's body back and forth on his cock. Billy's knuckles dragged along the deck. He turned his head to the side, encountered the man's bare foot, and pulled the man's big toe into his mouth. The man groaned and toe-fucked Billy's mouth in the same rhythm he was using to fuck Billy's channel with his cock.

Billy moaned and sighed, released the toe, and in a weak, fluttering voice, told the man how much he was enjoying the fuck, how arousing the length of him was. The rhythm picked up and Billy was being pumped faster and faster. His body flopped around as he was being taken more rapidly and with a frenzy that was making both him and his lover pant hard and groan and grunt with the exertion. With a weak cry of "Oh, Fuckkkk!" Billy ejaculated up the stranger's flat stomach and he felt his insides, almost simultaneously, being flooded again.

He was pulled off the man's cock and settled on the bed and turned toward the wall. He was so spent that he didn't even hear the man leave.

The next morning his eyes went from man to man, trying to discern who had visited him in the night. But he was unable to do so.

The experience had been so much different from the rough and cruel fucking he had been receiving—and had sought out—in the previous weeks, and it left him confused and pensive. It didn't seem less pleasurable than the full control and attack coupling he thought he had to have. His thoughts went back to the schoolmaster, Sam, and he thought perhaps he was beginning to understand what the man was saying about true lovemaking being an equal give and take.

It had not been that the previous night. But he was struck with the realization that, when he had awakened, his first thought was of wishing he'd had the opportunity to fuck the stranger as lovingly and completely as the stranger had fucked him. And the second realization that struck him was that he had not begged for punishment throughout the entire experience.

To collect and more deeply consider his thoughts on the matter, Billy volunteered to take to the crow's nest during the afternoon to spy for the sails of the other ships. Late in the afternoon, he did see sails. And when he saw them, the other vessel was near enough to him to make it out even though those below him on deck couldn't see anything.

"Ship Ho!" his voice rang out.

A chorus of "Where? Flag? Bearing?" rang out from below.

At that instant, though, he thought he recognized the ship. He believed it was the *Black Falcon*, the ship of his sexual master, Benjamin Palmer, Bloody Jack. The *Black Falcon* apparently had not seen them, though, as it was sailing a southwest course away from them.

It was an instant of decision. But Billy could not betray Ben. Or was it, he immediately wondered, that he knew that the *Elizabeth* would be no match for the *Black Falcon* and that he would be seeing Ben dispensing exactly the same carnage as the pirates the previous day had exacted before he realized that Billy was aboard?

He turned his body and called below, "North by Northwest, but the sails are nearly over the horizon."

This, unless the *Black Falcon* saw them would assure that the *Elizabeth*, and well ahead of it, the *Philadelphia* would maintain a course away from the *Black Falcon*.

He held his breath until the sails of the other vessel no longer were visible. And all of the time he was searching his brain for the answer of who he was protecting by the decision he had made.

That evening, a congenial captain's table supper over, during which Billy had searched the faces of all present for evidence of his secret lover, Billy retired early again. This time he was not exhausted. This time, he would be awake when his lover appeared and he would try the lovemaking on a completely equal basis.

But on this night, no one appeared in his cabin.

The next morning, all hands—not the Marines, of course—were put to swabbing the decks and preparing for a ship-shape docking in the Azores.

After hours of hard labor in the sun, Billy doused himself with a bucket of water and retreated into the corridor of the officer's cabins for a chance to cool down. A common sailor would not have thought of doing this, but Billy was treated like he owned the ship, and so could go where he wished.

Familiar sounds drew him to a half-open doorway of one of the officer's cabins. A naked Lieutenant Foster stood in the center of the room. He was gripping a wide-banded leather strap in front of him with a fist on either end. Bent over and suspended, feet off the ground, on his belly on this strap and nestled into Foster's groin, was the naked body of the cabin boy, Adam, his buttocks pressed into Foster's pelvis, and murmuring in a thick voice his total surrender to the fucking he was getting. Foster was slow pumping the small figure he held suspended in front of him, his eyes flashing his own enjoyment of the fuck. Foster would let the strap slacken and Adam's channel would slide down on the cock. Then Foster would tighten the strap back up, and the cock would slide back to the quick. A couple of inches of thick cock showed in the slacken cycle, and the sight of his cylinder and the hugely disparate sizes of the two men—and especially of Adam's small hole and the girth of what Foster had stuffed in it—made Billy gasp and give a deep moan. For his part, Adam was completely taken with the fucking he was getting.

Hearing Billy at the door, Foster turned his eyes in that direction. The lust therein did not slacken, although the pumping action slowly did.

No matter to Adam, however. He had already spilled his seed on the deck.

Foster slowly lowered the cabin boy to the deck, who turned on his back, spent, knees bent, still trembling and moaning. He was looking up at Foster with eyes full of awe as if the man were a god.

Foster stood there, strap still suspended between his fists, slightly panting from the exertion of the fuck. He was still in erection. Billy could see that his musculature was as magnificent as he had imagined. He also could see that Foster's chest had a dark down of curly hair swirling around the taut nipples and then trailing down his sternum, over his belly, and into his black bush. The cock was undersized in its spent condition, but it possibly was the thickest dick Billy had ever seen on a man.

So, this was what Adam meant by the strap, Billy thought. Not what he imagined at all. But arousing, very arousing.

Foster gave Billy a questioning look. He was smiling slightly, with a hint of a challenging sneer. He looked down at the strap, flicked it, and then looked up at Billy again, meaningfully. His cock already has hardening again, and growing in length.

Not a word was spoken as Billy untied his rope belt and let his shorts drop to the deck.

But then Foster spoke. "Is it true what they say? That you want it hard and rough?"

"Yes," Billy answered, feeling himself going hard at the mere mention of it.

Foster smiled and flicked the strap.

As Foster pulled Billy's ass on and off his short, thick cock—pleasing enough for Billy because of its girth and because it was long enough to pass his prostrate and because Foster had the power to ram it hard—and Adam looked up at the fucking with interest, Billy realized that Foster had not been the man of the night. He originally had rather thought he had been. The nocturnal lover had been smooth chested, and there was no doubt that his cock was long, if not thick.

Still, this Lieutenant Foster could fuck forever and provided a powerful ram.

* * * *

When they arrived in the Azores and the *Philadelphia*'s crew was being reassembled, Billy approached Captain Bainbridge.

"I have a favor to ask of you, Captain."

"Yes, what is it, son?" Bainbridge answered. He was beaming. His ship and crew had performed well, and the burden of responsibility was off his shoulders now. As soon as the *Philadelphia* was provisioned, it would be sailing into the Mediterranean.

"I wish to ship on the *Philadelphia*, sir. I wish to join the Navy."

"An admirable wish, sir," Bainbridge responded. "But officers are trained back at homeport, and you have the *Elizabeth* to husband until provisions can be made."

"My uncle has lawyers for the *Elizabeth* and it will be months before anything can be done. And my wish has always been to go to sea. As you've seen yourself, I have training for the life, and I'm a fast learner. And as far as being an officer, I don't ask that. I wish to sign on as a sailor."

Clearly pleased, the captain gave in without much resistance, although he did say, "We'll see how long without being an officer," as he could not fathom the nephew of a shipper working before the mast for long. The young man was small for the Navy and much too boyish looking for his own good—but it was true that he had shown talent for working in the rigging. Besides, his first officer, Lieutenant Foster, had suggested that the young man be recruited for the *Philadelphia*, if that was possible. And, Bainbridge reasoned, Foster was a sterling judge of men's talents.

Billy transferred to the *Philadelphia* and, although the captain agreed he should not eat with the officers, Bainbridge just could not countenance berthing Billy with the common sailors. He assigned him to a small cabin of his own with not much more room for anything but the berth.

The work of preparing the *Philadelphia* for sail again was harder than that of keeping her on the sea and, again, the crew was driven to exhaustion, Billy no less than the others. Even most of the officers were hard pressed. Foster was too senior for manual labor, but he kept form by taking the strap to either Adam or Billy at least once a day, an activity that neither raised objections to.

Billy was perplexed, though. If Foster had not been his lover of the night, who had been? It was an experience that Billy ached to enjoy again. It was much different from the punishing sex Billy assumed he must have. If sex like this was available to him, perhaps he did not need the danger and the punishment anymore.

He pined for a repeat but reasoned that everyone aboard was probably just as weary at night as he was.

The third night in port, he felt the man slip in beside him again and a hand start to move over his body. He reached over as well and took possession of the long, long cock. Both panted slightly as they worked each other's cock and mashed their lips together. The figure sank below Billy and he raised and spread his legs to give room for the face and tongue at his hole. Strong hands cupped his buttocks, raising his pelvis to the searching tongue.

Billy moaned as his buttocks dropped, the tongue was replaced by invading fingers, and the mouth closed over his cock. He writhed, begging, without heed, for a proper fuck, as the mouth and fingers continued working him until he had ejaculated and the lover of the night had swallowed his cum.

And then the figure was coming up from below him so that Billy was laying on top of the man, his head only coming up to between the man's muscular pecs.

"Dig in your heels and raise your hips. Give the cock length to fuck," a low voice growled.

Billy gladly did as instructed, more than ready for the cock. Still, he gasped at the long slide into him. There was no slow build to frenzy this time. The cock was pistoning his channel hard and deep. A fist was loosely encasing Billy's cock, which slid in and out with the rhythm and the power of the fuck up into him from below. He raised his arms and tried to pull the man's face down to his raised face for a kiss. But they just didn't reach. The man was too tall. Billy tried to turn his head to the side to reach a nipple with his mouth, with the same lack of success. That was when he noticed, however, that his cheek was rubbing against dense chest hair.

This was not the lover of the first night.

With a jerk the man spilled his seed deep inside Billy. Billy ejaculated again in the encased fist himself.

Billy collapsed on top of the tall, muscular body below him. The man was holding him tight against his chest. His cock was still fully encased, still deep inside Billy. It was throbbing, and there was every indication it would harden again quickly. This was a man of youthful vigor. But it was not the lover of the first night.

Both were panting hard, but that slowly receding—the man was recovering faster than Billy was. He was half hard already.

"Who are you? You are not the man of before."

"But the cocking is good enough for you isn't it?" the voice in the night growled.

"Yes, but . . ."

"There's no secret why others are at you. You're the best piece in the fuckin' Navy. I came to fuck, not to talk. And I will fuck until my cum trickles out of your ears."

Billy moaned at the image of that. This nocturnal lover already was more demanding than the earlier one had been.

"Roll over. On your knees. Now. We've got far to go before morning."

The man gave a guttural laugh, and Billy answered with another deep-throated moan.

With that, he pushed Billy off him, turned him, slapped him hard on the butt, put a heavily muscled arm under his belly and brought him up onto his knees, his head facing the head of the bed. Billy grabbed for the leather straps nailed to the wall above the top of the bed to aid with steadying oneself in stormy seas. These certainly were stormy seas.

The man crouched over Billy's raised buttocks, thrust hard and deep inside him, and began furiously riding his ass again. He was gripping Billy's waist with one hand and had snaked the other one around until he could grip Billy's cock again. He rode Billy hard to Billy's third jacking. But the man kept on riding. Billy's knees gave out and the man rode him down to the surface of the mattress.

Eventually, the man came again. He lowered his chest on Billy's back, and Billy felt once again how densely hairy it was.

This time the man was ready for lip work, and Billy dutifully turned his mouth to be taken brutally and possessively. Billy moaned as he felt the man go hard inside him once more.

It would be a long, taxing, glorious night.

But it was a different man. And the cock was almost as long, but again relatively thin, as the first man's. So it wasn't Foster either.

It had been great sex. Hard, yes, but not exactly rough. And certainly not punishing—not hurtful. And the man had thanked him for the four athletic ejaculations late in the night after he'd already taken full control—more, he had said, than any other sweet piece could give him—before leaving before dawn—enough before dawn that Billy couldn't identify him anymore than he could identify his first man of the night.

But who were they?

Chapter Five:

Off Tripoli, 1803

The passage of the Straits of Gibraltar into the Mediterranean two days following the visit of the second of Billy's night lovers was the occasion of much celebration on board. In keeping with naval tradition, Captain Bainbridge declared a half work day, double rum rations, and a festive meal for officers and sailors alike.

It was also the opportunity to haze, jestingly for popular sailors and somewhat more nastily for annoying ones, members of the crew who never before had made the passage. Billy's hazing was marked with making him walk the length of the deck naked with two heavy musket balls tied to his balls, pulling them low, and swinging against his legs until he managed to figure out a lumbering gait that minimized the bruising and entertained the sailors heartily. This strut was accompanied by whistles and yelled-out quips of what the gathered, more seasoned crew members would like to do with his body. The hazing for Billy didn't go farther than this, though. He was a popular member of the crew, most of whom dreamed of bedding him, and he quite clearly had been put off limits by a captain who favored him but was not of the proclivities of doing anything about it.

At the other end of the scale, the common sailor Jeb, a whiner, and one who was a sexual tease and delighted in setting one lover against another, was made to dress and make himself up as a woman as closely as what was available on the *Philadelphia* would permit and, after strutting his walk down the length of the deck, was carried into the forecastle and gang fucked by all who wanted to have a go at him and who had thought they had been slighted.

The cabin boy, Adam, had traversed Gibraltar on an earlier voyage and thus was exempt from the ceremony although there were many a sailor and Marine who might have been willing to put the traditions aside if Lieutenant Foster had not scotched their enthusiasm.

The festive spirit and the sexual innuendo of the day brought Billy's first nocturnal lover back to his room in the night hours. The two bodies came together in instantaneous heat, Billy having hoped for something like this, and knowing now that the lover was from the *Philadelphia* contingent and was someone who had been in the relief crew on the *Elizabeth*, where the lover had first appeared. Despite all of the sexual talk and the realization from earlier today that the sailors who had expressed their wish for a sexual coupling with Billy in various rough and exotic ways of mastering him, Billy was only now becoming aware that what underlay this was not jest and amusement at all but a barely contained desire to share him around in the forecastle and officers' quarters that was little different on the naval sailing vessel to what it had been on the *Elizabeth*.

It was an eye opener for him now to have confirmed that his nocturnal lover—or least the first one—was a U.S. naval man.

The two men were stretched alongside each other, using their hands to feel each other up to high arousal and each to center on the cock of the other. At length, the man rolled over on top of Billy, pushed his knees under Billy's buttocks, and entered his channel in a long, slow slide. He was holding Billy's torso off of the surface of the bed with a strong grip on Billy's waist, and Billy allowed his torso to go slack, with his arms dangling at his sides and the top of his head touching the surface of the mattress. He wanted all of the man, and his pelvis was raised to him so that his long cock got full purchase.

"To the root. All of it. Let me know if I must open more," Billy murmured.

"You have it all," was the low-voiced reply. "I wish there were more to give."

"Ahh, you are so long, so deep," Billy whimpered.

Billy sighed in the realization that this was the position with which the schoolmaster, Sam, had started to fuck him, and that memory increased Billy's pleasure. At a sound near the door, he turned his head and discerned that another figure was in the room. Another man, verified by Billy as his second, hirsute nocturnal visitor, sat on the bed beside the fucking pelvises. He reached for Billy's cock and started a slow pump while leaning over and kissing Billy on the lips.

"I would wish to be inside you too," he whispered as the kiss ended.

Without hesitation, Billy responded. "I would gladly give you suck."

There was a bit of hesitation now, but not for long. The hairier of the two lovers straddle Billy's chest and Billy sucked his cock to hardness.

He withdrew and sat by as the first lover changed positions, pulling Billy down until he was stretched out on the man's chest. He was encasing Billy's chest with his wrapped arms, holding him close, and spread Billy's legs wide but pushing them apart with his own legs. The hirsute lover was below them, kneeling between the spread legs. He helped insert the smooth lover's cock inside Billy's channel again, and ran his hands over the thighs and bellies of the coupling pair he was hovering over. Billy felt the cool wetness of a tongue running around the rim of his hole and the base of the other lover's cock. Billy's moans harmonized with those of the first lover. A hand found and slow pumped Billy's cock again, and then the hirsute man was covering Billy's cock with his mouth and bringing Billy to ejaculation.

Billy was still being pumped by the man underneath him and holding him close to his chest, when Billy felt the hirsute one crouching over his torso and coming in to possess his lips again. Billy could feel the hardness of the man's cock rubbing against his inner thigh.

Once more the man spoke to Billy after a deep kiss. "I would wish to be inside you too."

It dawned on Billy what the man was asking. "You mean at the same time?"

"If you think you can manage."

Both men's cocks were long but not particularly thick. Billy had been double fucked by two thick cocks before. He shuddered at the thought of the shared intimacy between three men of such a coupling—especially being done as sensually as this rather than in rage and as merely a symbol of superior mastery over a captive.

"Yes, please." He did no more than breathe the words, but his hirsute lover didn't ask again for permission. He was kneeling between the legs of the two men below; pulled one of Billy's legs up and to the side with a handhold on his ankle, providing further room for maneuver.

The man below started to moan as, with his other hand, the hirsute lover slowly slid his cock inside Billy's channel and above the already sheathed one. Billy began to pant, and his channel tried to expel the cocks by nature, but the second invader was preventing that with what he was doing with his hand. The man below loosened his grip on Billy's chest and went partially dormant while, encased at last, the hirsute lover began the pump of the fuck. Billy arched his back and pulled the face of the top man down to his and they kissed.

Because this was being done with both of his lovers showing concern for his pleasure and well-being, it became a deeply sensual and satisfying coupling for Billy, one that was to be taken up again in the ensuing days as the *Philadelphia* sailed toward the harbor of Tripoli to take up its blockade of the pirate port.

The dark lover asked, with concern, how Billy had fared.

"I would not want to miss having had this," Billy murmured.

"So we may share you in the future?"

Billy's heart soared. A future of being shared between these two muscular, virile men. "Yes, please. Again now, if you wish."

This was answered by a low laugh, "You are just as we have been told. The best lay on the Atlantic. I think you overestimate our stamina. Working in consort is exhausting."

When all three men had ejaculated, therefore, this was the last of the three-way fucking for that night. The first lover, having come twice, withdrew at some point, leaving the more vigorous of the two cocks taking Billy hard, standing on the floor and bending over the bed, and the man doggy fucking him from the rear.

"I want to build and best my four jackings of last time, if I can," the man growled in Billy's ear. "If you can stay with me."

The man could—and he could do it so well and so often and in so many sensual positions that Billy also could do his part.

Billy was on deck as the *Philadelphia* slid into place off the harbor at Tripoli. It seemed almost a nonevent. The crew and Marines of the *Philadelphia* and of the other two ships pulling into an arc off the Tripoli coast had been keyed up to expect opposition to the setting up of a barricade, but everything was placid as they did so. Four other U.S. naval ships, all within sight of each other, were arrayed farther out to sea so that there would be two nets set up to intercept any attempt to run the blockade.

The town of Tripoli certainly didn't look menacing to Billy. It looked like no other place that the young sailor had ever seen before. The land was barren, other than palm trees rising up between the houses, both of which were surprises to Billy. He'd never seen coastal land as bare as this or the exotic trees with green fronds fanning out above tall, slim trunks. And the houses were all a dull tan color by day as the town mounted a gentle slope from the harbor, but in the glow of the setting sun they would be luminous shades of red and orange and, in the twilight, a shimmering silver. They uniformly were flat roofed, but pencil-thin towers rose out of the townscape here and there, from which haunting chanting in a complicated foreign tongue wafted out over the water several times a day. One of the other sailors told Billy that this had something to do with the heathen religion of the residents. It all was quite exotic to Billy, though, and he took the chance whenever he could to cast his eye on the town.

The harbor was crowded with small craft, most of the vessels being no more than a fourth of the length of the *Philadelphia* and outfitted with triangular sails. Billy scoffed at how flimsy the craft looked, but the sailors told him not to be fooled—that the craft were swift and highly maneuverable and that many a merchant vessel had already been invested with a flurry of them and overwhelmed by the pirates they transported before they realized what was upon them.

It was there, in the harbor, where Billy could see the most activity. It was like a beehive, disturbed and buzzing angrily. This too, the sailors noted, was something that should not be ignored or cast off lightly. The Tripoli pirates did not at all appreciate the attempt to blockade their activities or to challenge their right to tribute for the rite of passage from the Atlantic into the Mediterranean.

Billy stood at the rail of the *Philadelphia* that first evening that the ship slipped into place off Tripoli. They were far away enough that a whole expanse of the coast opened to his gaze. But all but the town itself was just barren desert with an isolated mud-brick building and solitary palm tree dotted here and there. It was while the sun set and through the twilight and into the darkness of night that Billy was first to be mesmerized by how quickly and how often the visage of the town changed, with the change in the light. Even in the moonlight, it was a new setting, shimmering shades of silver and the slow, but relentless, flickering on of lights in the windows of the mud-brick buildings. He was unable to leave the change-of-light show even for his supper, a fact that Lieutenant Foster came up behind him at the rail and admonished him for in mocking tones.

"What shall we do with a sailor who fails to appear at the officers' table upon invitation?" he asked in a semiserious tone.

"I didn't think I'd be missed and the sights of the city are so intoxicating," Billy answered. It was then that he saw that the lieutenant was stripped to the waist, which even the officers often did in this climate when they were not on dress parade or at the supper table. Beyond that, Billy noticed that Foster had his strap dangling from one of his fists.

"It has been days since you visited me for your special exercises," the lieutenant said in a low, growly voice.

"We have been worked so hard coming into the coast. Perhaps tomorrow—"

"Perhaps right now," he growled in reply. "Come into this rope locker with me."

Foster backed through an open doorway into a rope locker and Billy followed him in. Moonlight streamed through the open doorway. Otherwise the locker was pitch black. The smell of tar matched the thickness of the atmosphere.

"Kneel."

As Billy did so, he heard the chafing of the unbuttoning of the fly in the lieutenant's trousers and felt the smooth linen of the material against his cheek as it was spread apart—and then the hardness of the flesh of the man's cock against his lips.

"Suck it."

When the ship's officer felt sufficiently prepared, he instructed Billy to strip off his own sailor's shorts, which he did, leaving him naked. He stood then, prepared to turn away from Foster, feel the strap go over his head and rest on his belly, and, after Foster's cock had been seated in his channel, the sensation of being bent over at the waist, his feet pulled off the deck by the pull of the strap on his belly, and having his channel pumped on the lieutenant's cock.

This isn't what happened, though. "Not that position. Something different. Face me. Lift your right leg to my hip and arch your back. Touch the floor with your hands, if you can." Billy was small and flexible. He managed to do as bid. He felt Foster crouch down a bit and then the man's cock come up between Billy's legs and into his channel. Now the strap came over his head and rested on his back, below his shoulder blades.

"I have your back supported with the strap now. Lift your other leg to my hip."

When Billy did so, he found he was suspended off the deck again, plastered to Foster's pelvis, Foster's cock inside him, and his torso held perpendicular to the officer's midsection by the support of the strap. The lieutenant began to pump, faster and faster, more frenziedly. He came with a grunt and a groan. As usual, Billy had already spilled his seed.

Letting Billy lower his feet to the deck and take the weight of his body back on himself, Foster declared, "There, that was good for you." It wasn't a question. It was the arrogance of the naval lieutenant speaking.

Billy didn't demure. It wasn't the loving his nocturnal lovers gave him, but he wouldn't disagree that it was good in its own right.

"You don't visit me often enough. You must remedy that."

"Yes, sir."

Then Foster was gone and Billy was pulling his sailor's shorts on again and moving out onto deck and to the rail to see what change nature had rendered to the light pattern over Tripoli in the twenty minutes he had been otherwise engaged. It was late in the night before he descended, with a sigh of having watched one of the wonders of the world, to his small cabin below.

He was followed into the cabin by one of his nocturnal lovers—the smooth one—who commenced a brief prelude of kissing and hand play, culminating in the remark during the exploration of Billy's ass with a tongue, "Someone has been in here already tonight, I taste," which was followed by a laugh and a slap on Billy's buttocks.

Soon the smooth lover was seated on the side of Billy's berth, with Billy, turned away from him, seated in his lap. The man was rocking back and forth, causing his deeply sheathed cock to work its magic on Billy's channel walls. Billy's head was turned up and toward the face of the taller man, and they were kissing.

"So many men inside you on the ship. Tell me what you like, what your favorite lover does for you."

"This. Always this. You and the one you share me with. Anything you do with me is the best."

A low laugh told Billy he had answered well. But there had been two laughs. Two different men.

Billy felt the hands of another on his thighs, and he shivered at the realization that both of his night-time lovers were there. A warm, wet mouth lowered itself over Billy's cock. The young sailor dug his heels into the deck, and he started to move his channel up and down on the smooth one's cock, sending his own cock into a slow fucking motion in the mouth of the hirsute one. The hairy lover was working Billy's cock well, and he was holding Billy's balls closely in the grip of a hand, rolling them between his fingers and pulling them out from Billy's body. The smooth one was swabbing Billy's tonsils with his tongue.

The hirsute lover squeezed Billy's balls, and the young sailor came in his throat.

The receiving lover rose up between the spread legs of the other two, and took Billy's mouth in a kiss that shared Billy's warm cum between the two. The kiss was brief, though, as the hirsute one moved his head over Billy's shoulder and shared the essence of Billy in a more lingering kiss with the smooth one, whose body twitched, and released its own seeding deep inside Billy's channel.

The hairy lover kissed Billy and rolled and pinched Billy's nipples between thumbs and forefingers while Billy ran his fingers through the hair on the man's chest and belly and did the same with the other's nipples. Billy could feel the insistence of the hirsute one's hard cock against his belly.

The three put their faces together as they were able for tongue flicking kisses, and Billy sighed and arched his back as the hirsute's lips went down to suck and nip at his nipples. Billy turned his face up for some tongue play with the smooth one, whose cock was hardening again inside the young sailor.

Billy moved his head aside for the two lovers to share lingering kisses over his shoulder and then the hirsute's mouth was at Billy's ear.

"May we? Again? May we share you?"

He had asked. Billy was being treated as an equal—just as the schoolmaster had said was the true mark of lovemaking.

"Yes, please. I want both of you inside me," Billy answered with a low moan. The moan lengthened into a groan and then into panting and small exclamations marking the second invasion of his channel, as the hirsute one moved his arms under Billy's thighs and lifted and spread them and crouched between the legs of the other two. He possessed Billy's mouth with his during the whole process while the smooth one flicked a tongue in one of Billy's ears.

The bulb of a long, hard cock was at Billy's entrance, and Billy reached down and guided it inside him, on top of the buried cock root of the smooth one, making sure that the first one stayed buried as the second one worked its way inside him.

All were holding-their-breath, tense, focused on the deep seating of the two long, hard cocks, accompanied by grunts and groans from all three—all three working equally to achieve a triangular unity. They held there, fully invested for almost a minute, their breath becoming regularized, seeking a syncopation of breathing.

Then the hirsute one started to pump. Not slowly, but frenetic almost from the beginning, joined shortly by the counter stroking of the smooth one. Billy's hips started in motion too. The three played a symphony, working to set a shared rhythm, then each briefly taking ascendance in driving the beat, and moving to a crescendo of each striving to be strongest, the most vigorous, the one driving the cocks the deepest possible inside Billy, and ending with three ejaculations, one after the other, and a collapse inward into one trembling mass.

Billy sat at the end of the berth and watched his two lovers writhe together on the mattress, wrestling with each other until they achieved a 69 position and, eventually, brought each other to another climax.

When the smooth one had left the cabin, Billy was on his knees on the bed, grabbing the straps over the head of the board, with the hirsute one crouched over him and pounding him hard. When the hairy lover had counted off his sixth jack off, Billy once more was alone.

By now Billy knew who his nocturnal lovers were. He thought he should have figured it out from the beginning. They had had too much energy and vigor, from the beginning, to have been the hard-working sailors on the ship. Their triangulation now was too close, too intimate for Billy not to be able to make out their features even in the darkest of night.

It didn't matter, though. It only mattered that they were there and that he was experiencing the glories of couplings of equality. There was still a bit of a way to go toward full equality in their fucking, though, as Billy realized the next night.

The smooth one, as always, coming to the cabin first, was flat on his back on the berth. Billy was straddling his hips and riding his cock, the two gazing into each other's eyes, sharing the flashes in their eyes as Billy changed the motion of his channel on the cock. The hirsute one came down on the bed behind Billy, his knees encasing the legs of the smooth one.

"May I share?" he whispered in Billy's ear. Ever the polite one about the double taking—in stark contrast to when he alone was taking Billy. In these instances, he growled commands, moved Billy's body at will and without request, Billy knowing it was all at the hirsute one's direction but also knowing that his lover would be concerned for Billy's pleasure too and would not cease the fucking until Billy was fully satiated.

In response, Billy turned his face back toward the hirsute one's, and they kissed while Billy's hips were being rolled up by strong hands, careful not to dislodge the cock of the smooth one, made easier because of the long length of both of the lovers, and a second cock was invading. Billy was stretched at this point, after several nights of doubling, so that the two cocks comfortably were accommodated and fit like a glove.

As the hirsute one took command of the plowing, Billy realized that the position he had taken with the smooth one— riding his pelvis—had been an unintentional statement of equality and perhaps, even, of Billy taking command. Once again, though, with the appearance of the hirsute one, control was taken out of Billy's hands.

It was a glorious fuck, the hirsute one pulling Billy's torso back to him, with arms laced under Billy's armpits, fists locked at the nape of Billy's neck, and the two kissings, while the smooth one played with Billy's nipples with both of his hands and held his cock hard but dormant as that of the hirsute one rubbed the full length of it in his plowing.

But it wasn't fully equal. Billy wished that it could be fully equal.

* * * *

Sunday was a day of rest—even on the *Philadelphia*—for most of the sailors when the ship too was at rest. In mid morning, with Billy trying to catch up on his rest in his berth, he rose to answer the light rap on his cabin door. In the corridor stood the two smiling Marine friends of Billy's: Hal, the blond, smooth one; Dirk, the dark, hirsute one. The two were smiling sheepishly, not sure if Billy would recognize them as his nocturnal lovers. But, of course, by now he had identified them for who they were.

He had already decided to complete the journey to total equality in coupling, and, though he welcomed them in, after a brief period of three-way arousal preparation, Billy declared that this time he would be voicing the commands.

He had the two Marines lie on their backs, Hal's head to the foot of the berth and Dirk's to the head, their legs entwined and their pelvises joined. The two hard cocks throbbed against each other. Billy, sitting on the edge of the bed next to the men's hips, took possession of both long, hardening cocks together, first with his encasing, slow-pumping hands and then with his mouth, to the extent possible pleasing both cocks with his tongue, teeth, and mouth cavity together.

Hal and Dirk, starting off amused and ready to accommodate Billy's demands, but not sure what he could do to give them more pleasure than they took for themselves, sank slowly into moans, slight movements of their hips, working of any part of Billy's body they could reach, and the occasional lacing of their own fingers together in acknowledgment of the shared experience.

When both were begging to be inside Billy, he climbed over and straddled their pelvises. Holding the two cocks together as one unit with his hand, Billy slowly sank his channel on the joined cocks and rode them together in what one of them described in a low, husky voice as a "camel moving in a wave across the desert" motion. Billy had no idea what a camel was, but he enjoyed the fucking as much as the two Marines did.

It was only after they were done with that, and each of the Marines had had Billy individually, with the smooth Hal taking Billy last, closely covering Billy from behind as Billy was bent over his berth—and with Dirk crouched over Hal from behind as well, with Hal fucking Billy and Dirk fucking Hal—that the two told Billy why they had visited him by day.

The disposition of the American naval forces was being changed. There was more action on the second ring of the blockade, with pirate ships trying to force their way into Tripoli harbor, than there was on the nearer line, where the *Philadelphia* was positioned and no ships as yet had tried to sail out of the harbor.

Thus the Marines were all being moved to the outer ring.

Although Billy missed not having his Marines to liven his nights and the next day had to seek Lieutenant Foster and his strap out for relief, he didn't have long to pine.

Almost as if the Tripoli pirates knew what was happening on the American naval vessels and the change in the balance of strength that was represented by the repositioning of the Marine forces to the outer ring that very evening, on Monday, October 31st, 1803, a date that Billy remembered also because it was his twentieth birthday, the pirates made their move.

Near twilight, six pirate craft started to sail slowly out of the harbor and seemingly into the arms of the first ring of American warships. The American warships went onto battle stations, with sailors such as Billy crawling up the rigging to unfurl the sails. The pirate ships milled around for a maddeningly long time, with the *Philadelphia*'s officers discussing among themselves why the pirates weren't trying to make a dash for it while the larger, more lumbering ships prepared to maneuver. But then the pirate vessels were on the move, breaking off two by two and sailing in different directions and at an angle to the American ships. It appeared that at least some of them were determined to make it through the blockade.

And then the *Philadelphia* was on the move also, sailing at an angle to close off access to the sea by two of the pirate ships, which, in answer, turned back toward the land. The *Philadelphia* continued sailing at them, eager for a first lesson to be taught to the primitive craft so that there would be no more attempts from the harbor to run the blockade. Bainbridge was discussing with Lieutenant Foster and another officer the pirates' mistake in not waiting for dark to try their flight, which would have given them an extra bit of leverage—when the ship shuddered and all aboard the *Philadelphia* heard and felt the sickening crunch of wood on sandbar.

The shallower pirate craft had maneuvered the lumbering *Philadelphia* onto ground, and had done so irrevocably so that the large warship was not going to be able to free itself.

The other American ships of the first barricade line, seeing what had happened to the *Philadelphia*, pulled back before they could be lured too far inshore as well. Then they stood off, hesitating too long to send off help on longboats, as pirate ships poured out of the harbor and swarmed around the *Philadelphia*. The sea was lit up as day by the flaming torches they bore.

The battle for the *Philadelphia*--or lack thereof--was over before full darkness had set in. Seeing the hopelessness of his position and that if he didn't capitulate soon the ship would be put to the torch, Captain Bainbridge commanded the striking of the American flag and the running up of a white flag of surrender.

The crew of the *Philadelphia* was standing in an uneasy double line when the commander of the pirates boarded the vessel. The surrender ceremony was formal, with Bainbridge making--and reiterating--only one demand: that all of his officers and crew be kept together until terms of ransom of the vessel and crew could be struck.

Billy was only later to understand the import of this demand--which, in any event, was not honored.

The crew was already being assessed and broken into smaller groups to be taken aboard the pirate vessels for the ride into Tripoli harbor before the evacuation of the vessel commenced.

When they reached shore, all were marched toward the entrance of the harbor fortress. Once in the entrance, though, they were separated into their small groups again and led off— already in chains to separate cells in the fortress.

Billy's group only consisted of Billy and the cabin boy, Adam.

They were barely in their small cell, with Billy chained to the wall by his wrists over his head and Adam staked to the stone floor by an ankle chain, when one of the Arab pirates, one of the leaders of the pirate attack, was standing between Billy's legs, holding them up and out with his hands and brutally fucking Billy against the stone wall, while two burly pirates were sharing Adam on the floor.

Chapter Six:

Tripoli, 1803–1804

For several days in the Tripoli harbor fortress prison cell, Billy and Adam were unchained to crouch on the floor to eat two mean meals a day and to go to a small, outside walled enclosure near the cell to piss, defecate, and stretch their legs. Drinking water was brought to them periodically throughout the day, mostly by the men who arrived to fuck them. A couple of times a day, each was doused with a bucket of water to clean the stench off them. Once they had lost the sailor's cut-off trousers and vests they'd worn at the dressing out on the day of the *Philadelphia*'s capture, Billy and Adam remained naked. Over time Billy was able to ascertain that it seemed to be some thirty pirates and local Tripoli soldiers to whose entertainment they had been relegated. He had no idea how any of the other members of the crew were faring.

After the first three days, he had to help Adam eat and hobble out to the relief yard. Billy had been steeled to this type of treatment. Adam clearly had not.

The last time Billy ever saw or heard of Adam was a week after they had been put in the cell—if Billy's reckoning of the passage of time by the periods of lightness and darkness and the counting of the calls to prayer that permeated the sounds of the town could be trusted.

Billy was chained to the wall and being fucked by one of the pirates, who was crouched between Billy's spread legs and supporting the crook of Billy's knees on his hips with his arms. Early on, Billy had decided that his best chance at survival and not being beaten, as the more cruel of Adam's assaulters were doing, was to make his assailants enjoy the fuck—and therefore want to treat Billy better. He made each man who took him believe that he had succumbed to their mastery and was pleased with the coupling. He would make the desired moans and groans and little vocal encouragements—learning ones in Arabic that impressed the Tripolians. He matched the rhythm of the fuck in the motion of his hips, and if the assailant wanted to possess his mouth during the fuck, he showed some enthusiasm.

Thus, the man fucking him was more involved in a sexual experience than just the fuck when a contingent of Arabs, dressed in long white robes that Billy later learned were called thawbs and were typically worn by Arab men, arrived. The man was alternating between kissing Billy on the mouth and leaning his face down and sucking on Billy's nipples during the fuck. And Billy was reacting as if this was the best experience he'd had in a fortnight.

The small group of officious-looking men were just passing by, but at hearing the sounds of more enthusiastic giving and receiving coming from the cell than they normally would expect, they paused and watched.

There was a leader among them, one who appeared to be about thirty, who obviously was well pampered and who was receiving deference from the rest. Rather than watching from the corridor, he drew inside the cell. The guards at either side of the door into the cell went into stiff attention, another sign of the importance of this man. He was tall and dark. His figure was thin, and both his bejeweled fingers and the toes in his costly looking leather sandals were long and sensuous in their movement. His fingers fluttered about his thawb as he watched the fucking—not just Billy and the one pirate at the wall, but also the two on the floor who had a limp, half dead Adam between them, with both of them sharing his channel. And his long toes scrunched up and then released in rhythm with the fucking of Billy. His piercing black eyes slitted in pleasure and his tongue darted out to lick his lips.

His retinue had entered the cell with him but held back close to the door, alert to exactly whatever his desire was. He motioned with his hand, and one of the men came to his side, lifted the hem of the man's thawb, ran a hand up underneath, and the puckering and undulating of the rich white material of the man's thawb at his groin revealed that his cock was receiving attention.

When the man was satisfied, the young man withdrew his hand and then the rest of his body to the back of the cell. Billy had come for the assaulting pirate in a spouting of cum and cries of awe and pleasure. Whether or not the response was feigned, it doesn't really matter. Billy had been initiated to the pleasure of the cruel and rough fuck.

Taking one last look at the tableau and then down at the men still sharing Adam's channel, the officious man turned and walked back into the corridor. There he spoke to one of the guards at the door, who left his post immediately, and shortly thereafter came back with the man Billy believed to be the cellblock commander.

After a short conversation, the officious man and his retinue moved on. But within an hour, Billy was being unchained, a clean, white thawb was being pulled down over his head, he was being blindfolded, and the hands of several men were picking him up and carrying him out of the cell.

He spoke what he hoped were words of assurance to the solitary figure of Adam on the floor, splayed out on his back, but there was no answering response from the young cabin boy.

* * * *

The new "home" for Billy, at least temporarily, was a palace on top of the rise from the harbor at Tripoli, or rather, a wing of *the* palace. He was surprised to find that there was more of Tripoli on the plain behind that rise than he had seen from the *Philadelphia* looking into the Tripoli harbor. In fact, he wouldn't be surprised to learn that Tripoli was even larger, in population certainly, than his own Boston. Tripoli wasn't just the name of the city; it also was the name of the ill-defined region.

There was no telling where most of the named "entities" in North Africa began and where they ended. They tended to be desert hinterlands of established cities. The only established boundary was the one toward the east, which separated Egypt from Tripoli. The Tripoli region took its name from the city on the western promontory of a scooped-out section of northern Africa, which also had a city, controlled by the Pasha of Tripoli, on the eastern promontory that was named Derne. To the west of Tripoli was another ill-defined territory around Tunis, and beyond that was Algiers, and beyond that, to the strait guarding the entrance to the Mediterranean from the Atlantic, was Morocco.

The pasha of Tripoli was a man named Yussif Karamanli. With the help of his younger brother, Mahmud, he had overthrown his elder brother Hamet, who was now in exile in Egypt, trying to build up support to return to power in Tripoli. The man who had seen Billy being fucked against the stone wall of his cell was the younger brother, Mahmud. And it was in Mahmud's wing of the palace that Billy was enslaved.

There was no better term for Billy's state at this time than enslaved. Unless it was "pet." Mahmud referred to Billy as his male wife, but Billy didn't really feel in such an exalted position as the man's spouse. Mahmud also collected and flew falcons for sport. Billy was treated no better or worse than those falcons. He was kept in the palace for Mahmud's occasional sport. Mahmud didn't make constant demands on Billy, because he also had wives he felt the duty to keep impregnated. But when he turned to Billy, he knew how to make the best of his sporting. He was an expert in and devotee of the Indian sexual positions of the Kamasutra. And, from this, opened up a whole new aspect of Billy's sex life.

Billy learned all of this not from Mahmud himself, but from the two Indian Eunuchs, Raatib and Fateen, who were assigned to keep Billy in shape and available whenever Mahmud called—and to train Billy to please Mahmud. The two referred to themselves as hijras, rather than eunuchs, and they assured Billy that they had willingly undergone the ceremony of nirwaan, which removed their penises, testicles, and scrotums, in India before traveling the world to offer their services to rulers with harems. Billy was not the first male wife, as they also referred to him, of Mahmud, and probably wouldn't be the last. Mahmud tended to have only one male as a wife at a time, however, they told him, in contrast to the many females he wedded and bedded and kept pregnant. Since a male wife could not bear sons, the eunuchs said, there was no particular reason to have more than one.

Being bisexual and dominating and pleasing lovers of both sexes was considered virile in the region. No one saw enslavement and forced sex, though, as different from "pleasing."

All of that said, Mahmud worked the male wife harder sexually than any one of the female wives—and he acquired most pleasure from the workings of the principles of the Kamasutra in his sexual dalliances with his male wife. It was much the flexibility that Billy had shown with the other man against the wall of his cell that had attracted Mahmud to him.

The hijras were chosen to watch over Billy constantly for the same reason ones of their kind watched over the women of Mahmud's harem—to ensure that the only cock inside Billy would be Mahmud's. Mahmud didn't call for Billy more than a few dozen times in the months Billy was enslaved by him. This was more than enough for most men, but Billy was used to having sex daily. This periodicity would have been very frustrating for one who had led the sex life that Billy had, if Raatib and Fateen had not shown that they could be adept at using their hands and fingers and in giving suck. Officially, such sexual practices didn't exist—unless they went with the penetration of the cock, so instances of such were overlooked, even though anyone in the court coming into the male harem when the eunuchs were servicing Billy could have seen that he could get as much arousal, pleasure, and ejaculation from their attentions as from Mahmud's cock. Although imprisoned, Billy was obviously supposed to be kept comfortable.

Thus, the two hijras, who had learned British English in their training, were able to satisfy Billy's curiosity within reason and to keep him from slipping over the edge of boredom in conversation and more stimulating ways, and they were polite, if strict with him.

They also were charged with keeping Billy fit, which met with Billy's desires, as well. Billy understood that an unmanned man could easily turn to fat. This was not so with Raatib and Fateen, however. They were experts in the sport of Pehlwani, a form of Indian wrestling, and in other Indian physical training routines. These included exercise with the dar nal, stone weights, and the gada club, which was heavy and was swung around in various ways and in pairs to help build muscle.

Mahmud was a devotee of these sports himself, and Billy was to attest that it helped build strength and endurance.

Raatib and Fateen were there also, because Mahmud was a devotee to the Kamasutra. Before he first sent for Billy, Raatib and Fateen schooled Billy in the many exotic positions that would be expected of him in the taking. So well schooled was Billy that, for the rest of his sexual life, he was unable to move into a sexual receiving position without thinking the name of the position in the gay male Kamasutra lexicon. He often found himself almost calling the positions out: Anvil, Swing, Reed, Butterfly, Tree, Octopus, Bamboo, Monkey, Missionary, The Wolf, Oyster, and so forth.

Billy's conditioning was not all sport, and there were pointed ways of reminding him that he was a slave. A couple of hours every morning, he was made to take a turn treading the pump device that raised water to the cistern in the palace courtyard. It was hard, back-breaking work, especially at the beginning, but it helped build and tone his leg muscles and keep his abdominals flat and ripped, for which he was grateful.

The first time Mahmud sent for Billy, he was brought before the pasha's brother bathed and scented and in a silky white thawb—but nothing else underneath. Mahmud was similarly clothed. Billy marked the great length of the man's fingers and toes. He'd heard that this signaled the length of the man's penis, and after having been fucked by Mahmud, Billy was able to express belief in the theory.

Raatib and Fateen were made to stand by, while Mahmud sat close beside Billy, the male wife's wrists shackled together, on the foot of his large, pillow-strewn bed. Mahmud held Billy close to him with one arm. The hand of the other arm went under the hem of Billy's thawb, and Mahmud slow pumped

Billy's cock to ejaculation while the man closely watched the expressions on Billy's face—which, as instructed, Billy tried to make as animated and pleasure-receiving as possible. Just before Billy ejaculated, Mahmud closed his mouth over the cock head and took the cum.

The hijras had told Billy he would do this—as he considered taking the other man's cum first gave him added power over the man and made him stronger. As schooled, Billy totally relaxed at this point, showing Mahmud he was in full control—and thus validating the belief.

"You will want to do this," Raatib had said. "You are a sensual man with a need for frequent attention, that is clearly recognized about you. He will be more the man inside you if his beliefs are supported. And he will call for you more often if he enjoys you."

"And the one man who wouldn't support it is no longer breathing," Fateen added darkly.

At this point Mahmud turned Billy over to Raatib and Fateen and called out seven position of the fuck he wanted to use that evening. They were to demonstrate with Billy that Billy could receive them as Mahmud wanted.

Having no cocks, the two hijras couldn't do what Mahmud could, but they could play the part well enough that Mahmud was breathing heavily and Billy too was trembling and was totally open for a cock that immediately thereafter and athletically thrust deep inside Billy in the Butterfly position— Mahmud in a sitting position on the bed, his legs extended, with Billy on top of him in a belly-up crab-walk position, Mahmud fucking in an up-thrust motion and his hands working Billy's nipples, penis, and balls—and transitioned quickly into the Anvil—Billy rolled up on his back with his legs running up Mahmud's torso and with Mahmud on his knees, stretched over Billy's body and rocking back and forth, letting his cock caress all of Billy's channel walls. Billy ejaculating twice more and Mahmud three times before they had reached the seventh position of Billy draped on the front of a standing Mahmud, his torso taut as a bow, with his fists locked behind Mahmud's neck, and Mahmud holding Billy's thighs outside him, while his cock rammed inside Billy's entrance again and again and again.

Mahmud always insisted on seven positions. When his senior wife conceived after that many positions when Mahmud was barely past puberty himself, she had birthed a son. And his next son was conceived from seven positions as well. He was a superstitious man, and he latched on the good omen of "seven" as his good fortune number in all matters. Then, naturally, all of his subsequent sons were conceived by seven positions as well, as he never again used fewer or more than seven.

Billy enjoyed the attention when Mahmud was there, and he did get release when Raatib and Fateen saw that he needed relief, but the sophistication and intensity of Mahmud's fucking was only accentuated by the relatively rare contact with him. Raatib assured him that the master called for him more than he had for any of his previous male wives, but this was little solace to the young man. Billy felt just like he thought one of the man's tethered falcons felt. Used to perfection but frequently ignored—and imprisoned in the intervals.

When Billy asked what had happened to the previous male wives, the eunuchs simply answered that he didn't want to know. All that they would say was that no man fucked by Mahmud was ever fucked by another man.

Billy's room was perched high in the palace, and he spent much of the time he wasn't treading the water wheel or honing his body with the Indian physical training exercises out on a balcony set with bars that gave him an extraordinary view of both the harbor and the hinterland. Whenever he heard unusual sounds from the city below, he would rush to the balcony to see if he could figure out what was happening.

Thus, when he was awakened in the predawn hour of February 6th, 1804, it wasn't just the orangish glow of the light on his chamber wall through the barred windows that sent him stumbling out onto the balcony but it was also the keening sound from the direction of the harbor.

It looked like the whole harbor area was in flames, but it only was the grounded superstructure of the Philadelphia standing still a bit off from the harbor. Two other vessels— appearing to be American Frigates—were sailing closer in toward the harbor than usual, and Billy only got to his perch in time to see longboats being hauled back aboard these vessels.

As would be revealed later, the Pasha of Tripoli had demanded not only a high ransom for the *Philadelphia* and its crew but also a significant increase of the annual tribute the United States would have to pay for its ships in the Mediterranean not to be molested by Tripoli pirates. President Jefferson had balked at this, and the pasha, in turn, had cut down the flagstaff at the U.S. consulate in the city. Of all things that had already passed, this was the first that traditionally called for a declaration of war, which Jefferson promptly had proclaimed. The firing of the stranded *Philadelphia* by its own government constituted a U.S. declaration of war on the pirates and pasha alike.

This in itself didn't appear to have much effect in the city or even on the Barbary pirates, as U.S. forces didn't attack Tripoli but maintained their blockade of the port. This didn't bother those in Tripoli all that much. The pirates shifted over to operating out of the second Tripoli port, Derne, across the scooped-out coast to the east.

But even Billy felt the ramifications of the event and the aftermath inside the palace. Rumors began to float in the city that the pasha had overstepped his capabilities. These were fueled by other rumors that the Americans, in addition to the French, were working on a plan to bring the elder Karamanli, Hamet, back to power in an assisted coup from his current exile in Egypt. Hamet was generally thought to be less despotic and cruel than the brother who had overthrown him.

Within months, Billy noticed extra guards in the areas of the palace he was permitted to see. There were other guards in this wing besides those of Mahmud, and the guards were taking a belligerent attitude toward each other.

"Mahmud is suspected of shifting his allegiance," Raatib whispered to Billy in response to his question about the tension in the air.

"But Hamet couldn't possibly trust Mahmud now," Fateen added. "Mahmud is feeling compromised either way he turns."

By now, Billy had become a trusted male wife—not trusted in the sense that he wasn't kept in his barred room and closely supervised by the two hijras, but trusted in that his chains were taken off at Mahmud's bed when he was summoned there and Raatib and Fateen no longer stayed in the bedchamber while Mahmud was performing his one suck, seven-position fuck routine with Billy. The release of the chains had allowed Mahmud move on to more intricate and demanding Kamasutra positions with Billy, and he seemed pleased that Billy, thus far, had managed to handle them all.

On an evening in late February, Mahmud was in a fifth position of taking Billy in the position of the Reed, in which Mahmud was crouched over Billy's body, facing him, with his arms under Billy's waist and pulling the young man's pelvis up to his cock, shifting Billy's weight to his shoulders, when Billy saw a figure moving in the shadows near the door to a balcony. Light flashed off the blade of the knife in the interloper's hand.

Instinctively, Billy rolled Mahmud's body away from the line of attack. This was so much not supposed to be something Billy was permitted to do in the very formally orchestrated sex session that Mahmud kept on rolling to the edge of the bed and came up with a short sword that had been hidden beneath the edge of the bed. He whipped around, prepared to run Billy through.

But Billy was already half way across the room, his discarded chain in his hands and looped around the neck of the assailant from behind. The failed assassin was dead before Mahmud reached the two struggling bodies to dispatch the assassin with his short sword.

All hell broke out that evening. A trembling "accomplice," bruised and battered, was thrust forward to claim that the plot against Mahmud's life had been perpetrated by the absent, deposed elder brother, Hamet. Mahmud accepted this explanation publically, but he could not shake the suspicion that the ruling brother, Pasha Yussif, had been attempting to cut down the number of possible pretenders to the position of Pasha of Tripoli. To add doubt to Mahmud's mind, someone set the whisper about that the executed assassin had been seen talking with Yussif.

Some said that the agents of the French in the palace helped to increase this suspicion as well as they could on the principal of "divide and conquer."

In fewer than three weeks, Mahmud precipitously set out into the desert on camels with his most precious possessions, striking for the second city of Derne, which had favored him in the past and would now, he hoped, shield him from both brothers equally.

Having saved his master, and having a proudly displayed bandage on a forearm that the assassin had managed to slice in his failed attempt to dislodge the strangling chain wielded by a body well-worked by the water treadmill, Indian sports, and physical training exercises, not to mention the strong and inventive cocking of Mahmud Karamanli, Billy had become one of Mahmud's prize possession. Only a few female wives were included in the entourage.

During the long ride over the desert from west to east, Billy learned exactly what the "waves on the sea" gait of a camel felt like.

Chapter Seven:

Derne, 1804

Mahmud Karamanli, and thus his captive male "wife," Billy, lived a much more Spartan and furtive existence in Derne than they had in Tripoli. Afraid for his life, and seeing plots all around him, Mahmud moved his pared-down retinue from one position in Derne to another location almost nightly. Mahmud couldn't trust anyone in the Karamanli clan now, not knowing whether the personal threat came from Yussif or Hamet—or possibly both. The brothers were from different wives, so Mahmud had purged his retinue of anyone not from his mother's family. The only two female wives he brought were from branches of his mother's family, as well. As their own fortunes—indeed, their very lives—were dependent on his well-being and power, they were the only female wives he could count on. Even the two hijras, Raatib and Fateen, were jettisoned, as they, basically, were in the employ of the Karamanli family.

Billy's world was reduced from a luxuriously appointed room with a balcony at the top of the Tripoli palace to an eight-foot by seven-foot collapsible cage in the corner of Mahmud's chamber of any given night that was erected after each move from one hiding place to another. Mahmud's falcons had a cage almost as large. Billy didn't need to cage to remind him that he was as much a prisoner here as he had been in Tripoli, even though he now was considered to be in favor and among Mahmud's trusted possessions.

A cot and piss pot was put in the cage for when Mahmud didn't have Billy out of the cage and in his own bed for the continuing tradition of the one suck and seven-position fuck. He was fairly frequently out of his cage, though, as Mahmud had only brought the two female wives of his mother's clan and felt the need to fuck once or twice a day in the fear that each day might be his last.

Fortunately for Billy's well-being, the situation came to a head fairly quickly.

An American plot to reinstall Hamet on the throne had already been set in motion. Within the context of the decision to burn the *Philadelphia* in Tripoli harbor, the former U.S. consul to Tunis, William Eaton, was sent to Egypt as naval agent to the Barbary states, with the mandate to back the claim in Tripoli of Hamet Karamanli. Once Hamet agreed to Eaton's plans, naval support from the naval frigates, the USS *Nautilus*, *Hornet*, and *Argus*, were pledged to Eaton's efforts by Commodore Samuel Barron, commander of the U.S. Mediterranean fleet. A detachment of ten U.S. Marines was assigned to Eaton, and these, in turn, recruited and trained some five hundred Arab and Greek mercenaries.

Once prepared, this force, the first land battle engagement force on foreign soil of the United States, started a five hundred-mile, fifty-day, march by foot and camels across the Libyan desert. The first objective was to secure the port city of Derne, and then the force would continue on to Tripoli, after which Hamet Karamanli's victory would be complete.

The first sign that Mahmud's household had that Derne was even less safe than they had anticipated was when it was evident that the pirate fleets that had relocated from Tripoli to Derne, always better informed than the palaces, were sailing out of the harbor and dispersing in all directions in the Mediterranean.

Billy was in his cage in the harbor fortress suite of rooms Mahmud was temporarily ensconced in when the informants arrived to tell him that the pirates had seen the *Nautilus*, *Hornet*, and *Argus* sail in close to the shore at the village of Bomba east from Derne on the coast. The pirates observed that there already was a land force occupying Bomba. Longboats had been launched from the ships, and the two forces had merged.

Distressed, but unsure of what the threat was—if it involved foreign naval vessels, it surely couldn't involve a plot by either of this brothers, Mahmud reasoned—the youngest Karamanli brother gathered his household and retreated up to the top of the town to the governor's palace. Here, he dithered in uncertainly and indecision for too long.

Hearing a cry of "The ships are here" broadcast from a nearby minaret rather than the anticipated periodic call to prayer, Mahmud was drawn to an upper window of the governor's palace on the morning of April 27th in time to see the first bursts of the bombardment by the *Nautilus*, *Hornet*, and *Argus* over the rooftops of Derne. After opening the falcons' cages and releasing his precious birds into the air over the city, Mahmud gathered only three nephews from his mother's family with him and fled the palace toward the western gate of the city—where half of the Arab and Greek mercenaries of Eaton's army were already pouring into the town.

There was a flurry of activity within the palace, and then all was quiet. Billy began working the hinges on his cage with the crude implements he'd managed to gather and hide over the previous two weeks expressly for this opportunity.

Once free, which took a while and made Billy feel that there may now be no chance of flight, he nonetheless remained calm. The worst that could happen to him would be that he would die today. And with the life he'd already led, that was a possibility on any given day. He felt fortunate to have lived so long. That sentiment having been offered up, however, he had no intention of volunteering for demise.

He had been naked. First, feeling even more naked without any weapon to defend himself if the palace was invaded in the next few minutes, Billy went to Mahmud's bed and retrieved one of several short swords the man had stashed under there for his own protection in the night. As he knelt by the bed, one of the cannonballs from the bombardment by the American frigates found a corner of the palace. He was flattened beside the bed by a blast that dumped part of the room's ceiling on top of the cage he'd so recently escaped from, flattening it to the floor. Large chunks of masonry had splattered across the room, missing Billy only because he had been crouching beside the opposite side of Mahmud's bed from the blast. Feeling doubly charmed at one blow, Billy was heartened to think that he was guaranteed at least one more personal miracle on this day. If Mahmud could have his seven fuck positions for good luck, Billy would gladly take three daily miracles.

Wailing from another room told Billy that Mahmud had abandoned his female wives too.

He stumbled through the debris on the floor to Mahmud's wardrobe and chose the smallest thawb and sandals he could find and shrugged into them as quickly as he could. Then he had the presence of mind to find windows on all four sides of the palace at the level he was on so that he could survey the best escape route. East and west clearly were both out. The land gates in each direction were the scene of bloody fighting, with the forces fighting their way into the city making headway. To the south was the poorer sector of the city, where the streets between buildings were mere walkways and the roofs more often were thatch instead of mud brick. This sector was already a fiery furnace, and no one was going in; everyone was stumbling out— into the armed melee in the city square beyond the façade of the governor's palace.

He found the wives, cowering in a corner alone. All of the male retainers Mahmud hadn't taken with him had left on their own. Billy told the women that their best hope was to go to the governor's wing of the palace and to try to merge with his harem—that there no longer was any safety for them on the streets of Derne, if there ever had been. He tried to tell them that any danger they were in would be from their own people, not from the American forces. They were too frightened to understand this, however, and Billy wasted precious minutes escorting them to the governor's wing himself, where they were taken in by an old, wizened woman, who Billy had to believe was the closest thing they could count on for protection and salvation.

Billy ran back to the windows at the top of the palace, knowing in his heart that he was too late to do much of anything for himself now as well. He could see that the fighting was already near the entrances of the palace itself—and he had to dive for cover as another cannonball landed on the palace. He hoped it hadn't landed on the governor's wing, but by the sound of it, it was possible that it had done so. It was clear that the palace was a target of both the land invaders and the bombardment from the sea.

The young American decided that his best bet for escape was at the harbor. He was a sailor. If he could commandeer a small craft, no matter how small—the smaller the better, actually—he stood a chance of escaping the city.

Looking down into the palace's central courtyard, he saw that there was a fair-sized pond in the center. And there was a watercourse leading from the southern, upper side of the palace to the pond and then streaming away in a channel again that went into a tunnel below the floor of the palace to the northern, down-slope side. The tunnel looked large enough to fit his relatively small body—the first time in years that he appreciated that he was small of stature. So that's where he headed.

He had to dispatch a man barring his way to the center courtyard, but he did so without knowing if the man was a palace guard or one of the invaders. All he knew for certain was that, wearing a thawb and with his dark coloring, he would, at first glance, be taken to be an Arab himself. He couldn't count on getting more than a first glance before someone tried to run him through—and the fineness of the thawb that he had pilfered from Mahmud's wardrobe would surely identify him as a patrician of the city and thus well worth the stab from various factions.

The water tunnel turned out to be tall enough and dry enough in the season for him to move through it with only his feet getting wet. At the other end, a good eight foot off the ground at that point, was a barred opening. Billy was still strong from his Indian physical training conditioning and imbued with enough adrenalin to give him superhuman strength—and the bars were rusted. He managed to punch them out and also to drop the eight feet without noticeable damage other than a slightly twisted knee.

It pained him to run, and he could do no more than lope awkwardly, but he was loping for his life, so he fought through the pain. He almost welcomed and enjoyed the pain of being active again—and free, if being an obvious target in a city under attack could be considered to be free. To him, it was, though. He was as free as the falcons that Mahmud had considered more important to give a chance at life than he did the man who had saved him from assassination in Tripoli. What happened to him now depended largely on his own ability and fate, he told himself, not on the controlling decisions of other men.

He made it half way down to the harbor before he was accosted by an Arab of the city who was more interested in ransacking a wine shop than saving his own hide. As Billy came into view, and possibly misconstruing Billy as the owner of the shop, the man was upon Billy with a bruising body blow almost before Billy saw him. Billy had been trying to move through the shadows of streets where no fighting was going on at the moment with the sole goal of getting to a boat of some sort in the harbor that he could handle by himself. He strongly felt both the limits and the glory of being entirely by himself in this endeavor. The streets in the area were almost deserted, the residents more than an hour ago having already moved up toward the higher city—where the fighting was now going on— to escape the initial bombardment of the lower town from the sea. Out of the jaws of the tiger and into the paws of the lion. He had to do what he could so as not to suffer the same fate.

The man was larger, and heavier than Billy. But Billy was in better shape. If he could only stay out of the grip of the big bruiser . . . but he couldn't. Billy made a feint at the man with the short sword, but the man had been holding a sack with stolen goods in it, which he swung just at the right time and sent the short sword clattering into the mouth of an alley. Billy backed toward the alley entrance, scrambling after the lost weapon, but the man was upon him, wrapping his arms around Billy, squeezing his waist and lifting him off the ground. Billy struck up with a fist, hitting the man under the chin and snapping his head back. But that proved to be a mistake, because when the man's head slammed forward again, he head butted Billy in the forehead. Billy collapsed, seeing stars, only momentarily, but it was enough time for the man to free one arm of the waist chokehold, pull a dagger from a sheath at his waist, and bring that up to slit Billy's throat.

It seemed to take an eternity for him to do it, though, and Billy watched the expression on the man's face turn from angry, victorious determination, to surprise, then confusion, and then, as blood began to run out of his mouth, to close down into a mask of death.

Billy didn't have time to extricate himself from the collapsing Arab before two men in uniform were grabbing his arms and legs and unbuttoning their flies as, carrying him between them, they pulled Billy into the alley.

Billy's thawb was bunched up under his armpits. One of the soldiers was bracing his back against the wall of the alley, with his knees slightly bent, and his arms wrapped around Billy's waist. Billy cried out as his channel was skewered on a long, hard cock. Then the other soldier was crouching in front of Billy and working another long, hard cock inside him on top of that of the first soldier.

Charged with the lust-raising adrenalin of hand-to-hand combat and with all three men panting hard and moaning in their three-way fuck, ejaculations came quickly to all three, Billy first. When the two others were finished with him, they let his body slowly sink to the ground.

"I see we came at a good time," Hal, the U.S. Marine, said, smiling down at a moaning, but quite satiated Billy.

"And how good it was to be able to come with you again," Dirk, the other U.S. Marine, said with a grin. "There's nothing like a good fight to get a man's juices going. We saw you and there was no question we both had to have you again. I've been hard since the fighting began. I see that Hal has been as well. We were actually coming into this quiet street to have at each other for a break."

Billy was about to comment, being dazed enough still from the head butt not to fully comprehend how his lovers of the night on the *Philadelphia* had magically reappeared near the Derne harbor in the heat of the battle. He was about to make a stab at commenting, though, when a whistle was heard and both

Marines stood up tall and turned their faces to the sound of the trilling.

"Ah, our commander, General Eaton, summons the Marine detachment," Dirk called out, and then he turned and started to move away.

Before he followed his comrade, Hal leaned down and said, "Stay right here and safe. We will come back for you when we can. I can't wait to hear what you are doing here. And, more important, I can't wait to fuck you again."

Billy moaned and closed his eyes. He scuttled a bit to the side, pulling himself further into the shadows of the alley.

But he would not have a moment's peace. A voice growled, "I wouldn't lay there if I were you," as a strong hand grabbed his upper arm and dragged him up into a half standing position, eliciting a groan from Billy when his twisted knee objected. Just as he was pulled away, a body, with blood covering the front of its thawb, landed on the spot where he had been trying to move too. He looked up, to see the face of a Greek. The battle for Derne had reached the rooftops.

As he tried to stand, his eyes reached the level of those of a big, black dog, its jowls covered in foamy drool. The word "freedom" entered his brain.

"I would have bothered you earlier, but you and those Marines seemed to be enjoying yourself. And there were two of them. One I could handle, but two would be a stretch. They handled you well, though. Do you do this with all of the men who accost you in battle?"

The pirate captain, Benjamin Palmer, a big grin on his face, was standing beside Billy.

"We three have a history," Billy replied. "What are you doing here?"

"This is where the Barbary pirates were, and I'm a pirate," Palmer said, his voice rife with tease. "I was leaving a bit later than the others because I wanted to check on what they might have left behind in their haste. I'd think you'd have remembered that I was a demanding pirate. I will have to see that you have reason to remember it. The more interesting question is what you are doing here—and in Arab mufti—but that can wait. My men are protecting a breach in the eastern wall.

But probably not for long. The *Black Falcon* is just down the coast. We'd best be off before the American frigates run out of cannonballs and decide to chase some pirates."

Chapter Eight:

Off Derne, 1804

Ben was taking Billy on an Oriental carpet on the deck of the captain's cabin in the *Black Falcon*. The position he was using was one that Billy knew was the Kamasutra position of the Reed, Billy's pelvis arched up to Ben's crotch from shoulders and feet on the floor, with Ben between his thighs and with a strong arm under Billy's waist, holding him up in an arch, as he was fucking him. Billy was sure that Ben would have no idea what the position was called—he would just do it as was natural—and because he knew this had been one of Billy's favorite positions.

Just as he wouldn't have known they were in the position of the Reed, Ben wouldn't know that he transitioned to a position known as the Stem, where he was on his knees but otherwise upright, and Billy was spread before him, weight on his shoulders, legs running up Ben's torso, and Billy pelvis lifted, with his buttocks resting on where Ben's thighs met his groin, while Ben mined his channel. This was a deep penetration position and Billy was panting hard and groaning deeply.

Ben had slapped Billy around a bit at the beginning of their lovemaking. Trying hard to remember, Billy wondered if Ben had been this physical with him two years earlier when they had sex in Boston. The more he thought about it, the more he thought that was so. This was when Billy wanted to feel controlled and punished for the guilt of having sex with men.

That was so long ago. He no longer felt the guilt. He now was looking for more affection.

He wondered if he had felt the pain of the blows in the same way then that he felt them now. Somehow he didn't think so.

He also wondered if Ben would fall into the seven-position routine that Mahmud had thought was natural and right. It would have both amazed and amused Billy to have such a different lover from Mahmud vindicate Mahmud's beliefs in that regard.

This was the fourth position Billy could identify—and that Ben probably couldn't—that just came naturally to Ben as a dominating position. It had started with Ben close behind Billy as they stood, naked, in the center of the cabin—the black mastiff, Freedom, watching them warily from his bed in the far corner of the cabin. Ben had one arm slung across Billy's chest, with his hand cupping Billy's chin and pulling the young man's head painfully. The fingers of his other hand were roughly forcing themselves between Billy's buttocks cheeks, and nearly lifting Billy off of the deck with the strength of upward thrusts. Billy knew there was no art in this; this just was where Billy was standing when Ben could not control his desires and needs anymore. He had invited Billy to the bed, but had not let Billy take a step in that direction before he was upon him—and inside him.

Billy was groaning and whimpering. It had been some months since he'd been worked like this. Mahmud had been too sophisticated in his sexual techniques to be this rough. When he was sufficiently aroused, Ben released the chin hold and commanded that Billy bend over, while standing, at the waist and grab his ankles. With his hands locked on either side of Billy's waist where the buttocks dipped in the waist, Ben thrust inside him brutally and began the fuck.

As he did so, he had growled. "I know this is a way you like it."

Billy almost murmured that this was known to Mahmud as the position of the Wolf—although Mahmud took it at a more sedate pace—but Ben would not have understood, and this was not a moment for talk. This had transitioned into what

122

Billy knew as the Greyhound, which was just a sophisticated word for what Ben also knew it to be: the doggy fuck.

Billy was not to know if Ben was headed for seven positions, or even knew of some of the more refined and athletic ones. During the fourth position, the Stem, Ben had arched over Billy's torso and his strong hands had taken a choke hold on Billy's throat. One, two, three chokes, in concert with three rhythmic short strokes inside Billy's ass with Ben's cock. Then a release on the throat, but a deep thrust of the cock. Repeated.

Billy gasped for air after the third release of the chokehold, only to find himself swallowing air and sputtering at the feel of the cock thrusting deep inside him.

After the third cycle, Billy coughed and rolled away from Ben. He lay there, gasping for several seconds, his hands going to his bruised throat. "I'm sorry, I can't," he mumbled, giving Ben a plaintive look.

Ben's own look was one of shock and disappointment. "You say you can't? You could before. You begged for punishment. You couldn't come without it. You've changed."

"I hadn't realized. But I think you're right. It's been some time since . . ."

"Two years. Can you have changed that much in two years?"

"I think when you're younger, you change more quickly . . . maybe?" Billy could tell that he wasn't saying something that Ben wanted to hear.

"I must always have been older then, because I haven't changed."

That statement was like a thunder clap in the cabin, the sensation of the closing of a heavy, oaken door.

After a few minutes, Ben rose from the floor and walked over to a stand with a flask of wine on it and a few crystal glasses. The top of the stand was configured to keep the glasses in place despite the rolling of the ship, which was sailing, Ben had said, west toward Algiers, where the foreign pirates were gathering until something was settled in Tripoli.

He poured two glasses of wine and walked over and handed one to Billy. Then he tossed off the wine in the other glass and returned to the stand for a refill. Without looking at

Billy, he said, "You are probably very tired. You may rest on the bed."

It was spoken more as a command than a suggestion or indulgence, so Billy picked himself painfully off the Oriental carpet and went over to the bed, took a drink of the wine, put the wine glass down on the bedside table, and then laid down on the bed on his back. But he bent and opened his legs, giving Ben what he hoped was an enticing invitation to come to the bed too.

Meanwhile, Ben had walked to the door of the cabin, opened it, and said something to the pirate standing guard outside. He walked over to the table with the charts on it then and studied those—or pretended to—without looking at Billy. Nothing spoken transpired between them either, as the minutes ticked away, the tension building until it was broken by Freedom noisily farting and huffing in his sleep in the corner.

The danger in the room was that Ben still was hard. Rock hard. Billy knew something had to be done about that.

"Ben, please. Come to the bed. Do what you will with me. I am yours totally—still." Billy moved up on the bed, his shoulder blades elevated on the pillows, and opened his legs wide, dug his heels into the bedspread, and rolled his pelvis up. He moved his hand down and spread his entrance with two fingers. If Ben would just turn his head, he would see Billy's entrance, willingly open to him.

Ben wasn't given time to respond to that invitation, nor did he look to the bed. There was a knock on the door to the cabin, Ben spoke a gruff "Come," and standing in the doorway, trembling, was a beautiful blond young man. Younger by a good three years than Billy's now nearly twenty-one years, and smaller and more delicate of build than Billy ever had been.

"Come, stand in the center of the room, Dieter. He looks young, doesn't he? As young as you were when you first came to me."

Billy's heart sank. That was probably more telling than his failure to respond to a punishing fuck as he once did. He no longer was as young as he once was.

Still trembling, long, thick, fluttering eyelashes cast at the deck, the young man shuffled into the room and stood in the center, on the Oriental carpet.

Ben circled him, a dagger in his hand. The young man was wearing silken knee britches, held up with a scarlet sash. It was obvious that he wasn't a sailor or a pirate. That only left captive from some conquest of a merchant vessel.

His skin was an alabaster hue—smooth, boyish, but well toned, pampered. He was sending mixed signals, which were more clear to Billy, who had had used several occasions to do this himself, than, Billy knew, to Ben, the arrogant self-possessed pirate chief. The innocent and boyish aspect Dieter was showing seemed false to Billy. He was overdoing it a bit. There were flashes of purpose in the eyes darting in snatches to take in the room, assess the atmosphere, and locating Ben as the man of power—the one able to give favor. Billy knew Ben would not be able to see this. Billy himself only was able to do so, because he had had to do this himself. Indeed, he had done so with Ben the first time, being brought to him as a disposable captive, knowing he wanted Ben's cock inside him, but knowing that Ben needed to see him as hesitant and vulnerable for his own pleasure. A pirate, like a general, needs to conquer, to take something from the other by force. Something told Billy Dieter was fully aware of this—and that Dieter was a survivor—and, Billy could tell, a user.

Billy held his breath. He felt like his life was being relived—that Ben was making him watch what they once had had but that now seemed to be lost to them.

"Dieter here is a very recent prize of mine," Ben said to no one in particular, as he came up behind the young man and embraced him. The young man whimpered as Ben lifted his chin and took the young man's full lips in his for a brief kiss.

"You remember when you were brought to me as a prize—and what I did with you, don't you, Billy?"

Billy answered with a "yes," but it didn't seem like Ben was listening for an answer. Rather, he was sending a signal of the event to come.

"I debauched you to within in inch of your life. I reamed you to twice your channel width. Again and again."

Ben was looking at Dieter for a response. There was a sob, not more. Nothing to assure Billy that Dieter even understood English.

In any event, Billy knew Ben wasn't bragging. That was exactly what he had done that first time. Billy remembered Ben being amazed that Billy was still alive after it was over—that apparently not being a requirement for Ben's ritual with young captives. That marked the start of their long arrangement. Billy had been able to take it, and Ben had needed that sort of taking. Total pillage and victory; nothing less.

"I acquired him from a German merchant ship making a run for Egypt. It didn't get there. Dieter isn't a virgin. He was servicing men on the merchant ship, I am sure. He says no, but I cannot believe he would have been left untouched. And my men got to him before I discovered him. But no man will master him as I will do. Do you not believe that, Dieter?"

Dieter acted like he didn't know he was being asked a question. Billy now thought otherwise. There was a certain calculation in the eyes that betrayed him.

"Has any man who has ridden you had the cock and balls I have? Has any man ridden you for three hours or more?"

Billy looked to Dieter for signs that he thought this an exaggeration. Billy knew it wasn't. Dieter just gave Ben a wild-eyed look, indicating now that he knew he was being addressed and that he was expected to provide some response, but at least wanting to leave the understanding that he had no idea what the American pirate had said—but that, whatever it was, it frightened him.

Ben's massive erection would have been a bit hard to ignore, though.

Billy watched, seeing his early life flashing before his eyes, his own subterfuge when being taken by Ben the first time—of his fight, when subterfuge failed him, to survive the hours of brutal taking and his surprise when he had managed to do that—his desire thereafter to have this from Ben each time. Billy had fought for as long as he could, which wasn't long, and which only seemed to energize Ben more, and which ended only with Ben fully encased in Billy and Billy realizing there was nothing of him left to defend, only an ordeal to try to survive.

And then the ordeal transitioning to a heaven like he'd never known before, of a cock throbbing deep inside his gut and flooding him again and again.

Dieter evidently was taking another route. He showed Ben that he accepted the pirate chief as his master and the inevitability of his taking by lowering his eyes and giving a small, studied sob.

As it often had with Billy, the session started with Ben holding the diminutive Dieter close to him from behind and moving the blade of the dagger under the scarlet sash, cutting it, and then carefully cutting the silken breeches off Dieter's legs, not even creasing the soft flesh underneath. Still holding the young German painfully close to him with one arm, Ben pumped Dieter's pert little cock with a fist in a progressively faster beat until the German youth ejaculated with a groan and a moan.

Ben laughed when Dieter came, and said in a low-pitched, smug voice, "We will have it all now just in case anyone before me has neglected you in any way; in case anyone before me has left any part of your experience unmastered. This will be your total taking, and you will long remember it—and regret not having it when a lesser man than me is fucking you—if, of course, you survive it. I care neither way. You were as good as dead when you were taken captive—and would have been earlier if I had not pulled you way from my sailors."

There was no obvious reaction from Dieter on his possible demise in this process. Billy took this as a sign that the German youth retained hope he could control the situation.

Billy remembered, with a start, that Ben had done the same to him, said the same to him that first time of theirs. Once again Billy had the impression that this all was more for him—more a mourning of the change between them—than for either Dieter's undoing or Ben's pleasure.

Ben pushed Dieter onto his back on the Oriental carpet then, and with a knee pinning the young man's sternum to the floor, worked his channel with a thick, greased wooden dildo, as Dieter groaned and cried at the indignity and claimed pain.

Billy knew this was a mercy, though. Ben was conditioning the young man's channel to take the thick, long, hard phallus still rising up from his reddish bush, looking more angry, more demanding than ever before. Still, Billy wondered how such a small figure as Dieter was ever going to be able to manage Ben. He had, however, and he was not any larger in stature as Dieter was. He knew that Ben was doing this for him, really, showing him what they'd had, taunting him with it. There was nothing that either of them could do about that, though. Time had moved on. Billy was older now—and had acquired other experiences, more refined tastes. He didn't need what Ben gave to take his pleasure to the heights now. It was Ben who had not grown up.

But there also was nothing that Billy could do for Dieter, even though the young German looked over at Billy with pleading eyes during the initial fucking that almost—almost—was convincing. Despite the subterfuge, Billy knew that Dieter would have to endure almost more than he could take. However, Billy well remembered the passion and pleasure of it too. He half expected that Dieter, like him, would be begging for it—again and again—before the session was over.

Unless Billy missed count, when the actual fucking started, there were only six position changes before Ben first ejaculated, so there was no verification of Mahmud's seven-position theory. But what came closest to upsetting Billy in this more than an hour of coupling was that Ben was using more sophisticated Kamasutra positions with Dieter than he had used earlier with Billy.

To stop all wondering, after working the young man's ass with the greased dildo, Ben had lifted Dieter and slammed him down on his back on top of the maps on the chart table, pushed his legs between Dieter's thighs, and leaned down and taken Dieter's mouth with his in brutal kiss. Dieter had pounded on Ben's chest with his small fists and writhed underneath him, showing signs of fight now—sensing, Billy was sure, that this was what Ben wanted from him—and Ben had risen off him, backhanded him across the mouth and laughed. Taking Dieter's throat in a choke hold with one hand, Ben presented his cock to the young man's hole with the other. Dieter screamed and tore without effect at Ben's choking hand with both of his hands as Ben's cock worked its way into the tight channel. The struggle continued with Dieter ineffectually fighting Ben until Ben's cock was fully saddled. Then Ben took his hand away from Dieter's throat and hovered over him, the heels of his hands pressed on the desk at either side of Deiter's torso. Dieter was silent, his body unmoving, other than his heavy panting and his whistling of a continuous, low whimpering sound.

"There then, little one," Ben said in a low, hoarse voice. "You may have had other men's cocks in you, but none like mine. And none can dominate you as I can. Now we begin. Whatever has come before, you will remember this as the first real time. Remember me throbbing here deep inside you as the watershed between any semblance of your innocence and your total taking by a real man."

They held there, as Ben had done for me, for more than a full minute, Ben fully saddled and Dieter panting and whimpering, fully possessed. Dieter shuddered and moaned as, at length, Ben moved his cocked, just a fraction of an inch, in and out, in and out, deep inside Dieter's gut.

Then Dieter cried out and struck at Ben's chest again with his little fists as Ben began to pump harder and with broader strokes. The pumping went on, though, and Ben laughed, pleased by Dieter's attempt at a defense. Dieter shot a small load out of an undersized cock, and then just collapsed under Ben, his arms out flat on the table and his face turned aside, staring at Billy, as Ben pumped on. At the moment of Ben's ejaculation, Billy felt his own suspicions completely vindicated in the flash of victory he saw in Dieter's eyes. And it was a victory he was flashing at Billy. Billy understood then that Dieter had seen Billy as the danger in the room. The competition.

"There. It is done. Marked as mine now," Ben said, full of satisfaction.

Again the little flash of victory telescoped by Dieter's eyes in Billy's direction.

Ben pulled off Dieter's docile body and went over and poured himself another glass of wine. Dieter didn't move, laying askew on the table as Ben had left him and panting shallowly. Billy thought Ben the fool then. He would see Dieter's position as unvolunteered, but total surrender. Billy saw it as a mark of the young man's victory. And Billy understood it as a victory over him as much as over Ben.

"Now that there is no reason to fight me anymore, nothing to protect, we will start the fucking of our little German playmate in earnest—when I've been fortified a bit by the wine."

Billy took that as an indication of the depth of Ben's displeasure with him and with the situation both found themselves in, a displeasure he couldn't voice, because, at the base, Billy understand—and Ben must have, at least almost—understood that this all was in grief over the changed relationship between Ben and Billy. It had little to do with Dieter—at least for now. Billy knew Dieter would work hard to change that. And he feared that Dieter was clever enough to win.

There was no reaction by Dieter to Ben's statement of trials to come. Billy thought this was a misplaying of the German's hand, but he was also a bit dismayed that Ben seemed too blind to the game being played here to catch the gaff.

When the fucking session started in earnest, Ben began by having Dieter in the position of the Bamboo, with Dieter on his back on the Oriental rug, with Ben crouched between the young German's thighs. One of Dieter's legs ran up Ben's torso, and Ben had Dieter's buttocks raised on the side but pushing it up with a knee. In this position one wall of Dieter's channel was getting the most attention. The other side of the channel then had its turn when Ben reversed sides. Dieter became increasingly involved in the fuck, not taking long either to show that he wanted what Ben was giving him but also that he wasn't the naïve young near virgin that he had exhibited.

Before long Dieter was sitting on Ben's cock and moving through positions, seemingly on his own, including one called the Swing, another the reverse Bonobo, with Ben sitting up, with Dieter riding his cock, facing away from him, and Ben lifting the spreading the young man's legs with his arms. The modified Scissors position is where Dieter was choked into semiconsciousness. Dieter was sitting on Ben's cock, with Ben on his back and Dieter facing him, and Ben pushed Dieter onto his back, swung his legs up to where they had a grip on Dieter's throat and choked him into gagging near-unconsciousness.

Billy couldn't help himself. He cried out when it looked like Ben was going too far and that the young German would perish. Ben released Dieter then, who remained quivering and coughing on the Oriental carpet, and Ben went and refilled his wine glass. He turned to Billy then, and with a voice that seemed to have tinges of both regret and dismissal in it, spoke to the young man who had been his lover.

"I'll have one of the men show you to a small cabin of your own that you can have. You can spend your days here with Freedom and me. You may take a lover from anyone on board as you wish. I know you cannot live without the cock."

He had opened the door and spoke to the guard. He turned to Billy and looked expectant. He was trying to be cold, but Billy knew Ben well enough to know that he was finding this painful. Billy rose off the bed and picked up and shrugged on the thawb that he had been wearing until they had boarded the ship and that Ben had taken off Billy as soon as they had entered his cabin, unwilling and unable to wait to commence the coupling. At the door, Billy turned, to see that Ben was lifting Dieter up from the deck and carrying him to the bed.

Perhaps Mahmud was right after all, Billy thought as he followed the guard to his cramped, but private, cabin below. Perhaps they would reach seven positions this evening—and perhaps more. It had seemed impossible that Dieter's channel could accommodate Ben, but it hadn't taken Dieter long not only to manage that but also to participate fully in the coupling.

Billy didn't feel sorry for Dieter. When he'd been where Dieter was, there was no question that Ben was controlling him. Perhaps Ben was showing signs of growing older too. It certainly looked like Dieter was exercising a full share of control.

Chapter Nine:

Algiers, 1804 and 1815

The harbor at Algiers seemed almost to disappear altogether as the pirate ships moved into the deep-water port right up to the dock and then, when there was no more room at the docks, right up against the ship between them and the dock—and so on until the whole surface of the space between the two headlands encasing the harbor was just one continuous deck with a forest of masts.

Many of the vessels were part of a confederation that was forming to control the Mediterranean, all under the command of a towering pirate chief of indeterminate nationality who was called Khair ad-din, spoken of by that name because of his similarities to the sixteenth-century Turkish admiral and scourge of the Mediterranean, Barbarossa, whose real name—or so it was rumored—had been Khair ad-din.

The *Black Falcon* was lashed to Khair ad-din's ship, and the two pirate captains took to each other immediately. They both fancied themselves as superb card sharks, both enjoying various forms of poker. While they sat out events in the fight for Tripoli through the remainder of 1804 and into the next year, the two settled into high-stakes card games every other evening, one evening on Khair ad-din's ship and the other on the *Black Falcon*, with a day in between each meeting for whoever lost the worst to steal his next stake from under the nose of some other pirate in port. Both Billy and Dieter were permitted to attend these games, but they sat in the background—which didn't mean that they didn't get a full share of attention. Billy was twenty-one now, but still youthful looking and with a sensuality that made men gravitate to him and dream. Dieter claimed to be nineteen, but Billy wouldn't have been surprised if he was shaving a year or two off.

While banned from Ben's bed—temporarily, Billy hoped—he had been with a progression of lovers on the *Black Falcon*. A new generation of young Arab and Turkish pirates had come forth in the last decade as the pirates of old from the New World began to fade away. Having been with Mahmud Karamanli, Billy now had a taste for Mediterranean men. And, on the *Black Falcon*, he had come to know that now he enjoyed men who were younger than him, virile and vigorous, and with finely toned bodies. Unfortunately, there weren't too many pirates that met these preferences, as yet. But there were enough on board the *Black Falcon* to keep Billy well cocked. And, for their part, the young Arab and Turkish pirates were happy for the chance to fuck Billy as long as their pirate chief did not cut off their balls for doing so and remained crazy enough not to touch Billy sexually himself.

One night in early 1805, Billy had felt unwell after supper and had not gone over to Khair ad-din's ship for the usual evening of card play. It had just been a passing indigestion, though, and he was feeling quite well enough within an hour to seek out the newest member of the crew, a young, strapping Turk, and was laying, splayed and drowsy and quite satisfied on his back on his berth with the cum inside his channel still warm, when Ben appeared at his cabin door.

Billy didn't like the almost apologetic look Ben was giving him.

"Gather your things, Billy. You are transferring over to Khair ad-din's ship."

He had said it with a soft voice, but it had hit Billy like a whip crack. Ben was looking everywhere in the cabin but at Billy.

"You should feel privileged. Khair ad-din insisted that you be put up for a bet. And he won. He won you in a card game."

Billy waited, breathless, for Ben to say that he would win him back at the next game. But he waited in vain for Ben to say that.

As Billy came out into the gangway with his kit, Dieter was standing in the distance, looking very pleased with himself about something. Billy wondered then if Dieter had suggested to Ben what he could use him as his stake in the card game when Billy hadn't gone over to the other ship with them. He further wondered at the possible origin of his brief indisposition following supper.

Khair ad-din, a heavily tattooed and battle scarred giant with a massive chest and equally proportioned elsewhere with a strong hint of Turkic genes, was a master of the Kamasutra positions. Billy was exhausted that night, when the session was completed with the elite position of the Monkey, with Khair ad-din on his back, legs folded up almost to his chest, Billy sitting on his cock and buttocks, facing away from him, with Khair ad-din's huge feet flat on Billy's shoulder blades, his hands gripping Billy's wrists and pulling Billy's arms back. Both of their pelvises were in motion and both were moaning their pleasure as Khair ad-din's cock mined Billy's depths deeper than any other man had reached.

"The highest prize I have ever won in a card game," Khair had whispered to him as they were in a short cooling-off embrace before Khair thrust inside him again.

Clearly pleased with Billy's expertise at the sophisticated arts of the male Kamasutra positions, Khair ad-din kept Billy with him in his bed that night. Billy suspected that Khair ad-din also adhered to Mahmud Karamanli's seven-position ideal—but that he thought that double the ideal in a night was the best luck of all.

The next day, Billy was taken below in Khair ad-din's ship and locked in an eight-by-ten foot cage with a cot and a pisspot. He was told he was being thus imprisoned not because he displeased Khair ad-din, but because the pirate chief couldn't trust his men to keep their hands off Billy, and he didn't want to have to hang any of his crew from the yardarm for something they couldn't resist. Many were the nights, though, that Billy spent in Khair ad-din's bed rather than in the cage.

Later in the year of 1805, all of the maneuvering in Tripoli came to naught. The United States struck a treaty with Yussif Karamanli that lifted the blockade of Tripoli, handed Derne back to the pasha, included ransom to the tune of $60,000 for the hulk of the *Philadelphia*, settled that much more for the ransom of all of the *Philadelphia*'s crew that still survived and could be produced, and recommenced a new system of tribute, albeit at a reduced rate, to protect Mediterranean shipping from the Tripoli pirates, with the pirates toning down but not completely abandoning their activities.

Hamet Karamanli slipped out of Derne and made his way back to his Egyptian exile. Mahmud Karamanli didn't surface and was never again mentioned as a factor or a problem in the Tripoli pasha succession.

The blockade no longer needed, the U.S. frigates and other naval vessels went back to sea, clearly headed for Algiers—and the pirates congregating in Algiers fled before them, Khair ad-din's vessel and the *Black Falcon* taking off in different directions.

* * * *

Billy was with Khair ad-din for nearly twelve years. In that time Billy had no other lover—not because he would not have liked variety and even, in the earlier years, greater frequency, nor that men did not continue to find him desirable, but because Khair ad-din limited the opportunity. No other man near to Khair ad-din—and thus to Billy—dared cross the pirate chief.

The first several months were intense in their lovemaking, and Billy was content, finding the pirate chief solicitous, vigorous, expert, and hugely endowed enough to keep Billy satisfied. As fearful and brutal a fighter Khair ad-din was in the Mediterranean, he was refined in bed. But over the years, slowly, as with any committed couple, the sexual passion became less and the need for companionship and shared experiences and counsel grew.

For nearly a year, Billy was kept in his cage in the ship's hold whenever he wasn't with Khair ad-din, and Billy lived in the despondency—except when he was lying under Khair ad-din—that his life seemed to be one of moving from one man's cage to the next. After that year, though, he was spending more and more time with Khair ad-din in the captain's cabin.

The pirate master's vessel only rarely left Algiers harbor once the Americans became weary of chasing pirates in the Mediterranean and pulled the bulk of their navy back nearer their own shores. Difficulties with the British that culminated in the War of 1812 had increased on the Atlantic coast. Khair ad-din tended to have the many pirate vessels under his command sail out from Algiers at his direction and then sail back to him with his share of the booty.

Thus it was on one afternoon when Khair ad-din was performing the position of the Tree on Billy on the exercise mat in the captain's cabin, with Billy on his back and the pirate captain crouched below his pelvis, raising Billy's entrance to his gently plowing cock while Billy had one foot resting on the pirate's breast and Khair ad-din was holding Billy's other leg to his hip, that, between grunts, Khair ad-din said, "We go on the prowl tomorrow. You will be in the cage more."

"Why?" Billy responded. "What is the need for that? Surely you trust me enough now—I would not lie with another man. Can we not get rid of the cage? And can I not just become a pirate like the rest?"

"You are too small, little one," was Khair ad-din's reply. Then he grinned and said, "You also are not ugly enough to be a pirate. You would be too much of a distraction."

This seemed always to be the response to Billy's desire to become a pirate—all the way back to when it had been Benjamin Palmer's answer as well.

Seeing that Billy looked hurt, the pirate captain changed to the position of the Yin and Yang, where he sat, legs crossed in a yoga position and Billy sat facing him, buttocks on the larger man's thighs, Khair ad-din's cock buried deep inside Billy's channel, and Billy's legs wrapped around the pirate chief's waist. In this most intimate position between the two, a position Khair ad-din reserved for when they were closest, most affectionate with each other, Billy rubbed the other man's nipples with his hands and let his fingers trace the tattooing and battle scars on the pirate's chest, while the pirate held Billy close with one arm, worked Billy's cock with the other, and rocked both of them back and forth, thus giving Billy's channel deep attention with the cock.

"I know you are strong and adept—for your size— Billy," Khair ad-din murmured when he felt Billy relax in this position and heard his sighs of sexual pleasure. "There was a seriousness to what I said about being ugly. You could handle one pirate trying to take you, but not three, and they would come in groups—and take you in groups."

"I have done that before—and enjoyed it," Billy whispered, but he quickly continued, "Not that I would want that anymore. You are all I need."

"You are not as young as you were when you were entertaining groups of rough men," the pirate answered. "And there is another reason why you cannot become a pirate and why you have to be locked in the cage much of the time we are at sea."

Billy didn't respond. He didn't want to hear any such reason.

So Khair ad-din continued without the invitation to do so. "I am ready to be lost myself—much of my life has been lived as if that was the day I would die. A pirate can do no other. And that's another reason I cannot let you become a pirate. I cannot bear the thought of any day being your last. So, if we become engaged in battle, you will be in the hold, in the cage, dressed as a merchantman, and able to say you are a captive, not a pirate."

"But . . ."

"And that would be the truth. You have ever been the captive here, make no mistake about that. You are here because I want you, and for no reason you have selected. You are here for me to fuck—and for no other man. You keep me vigorous, and I must have a man to fuck apart from the others. To take one or more of the crew as a lover would cause dissension. You are here because you are convenient. The truth is hard but there it is. You stay here because you have learned the Kamasutra positions, though." He laughed then, obviously attempting to take the edge off the hard truth. Seeing that Billy refused to be amused, though, he ended with more of the truth. "If you had not pleased my cock so, you would be dead now. And I would have another man in my bed, probably a young, handsome man like you—but younger—until I was tired of him."

Billy rather thought there was a great deal more involved now than this—that he wasn't just a sexual toy for the pirate chief. He wondered if Khair ad-din genuinely didn't realize that after more than ten years, the two were much more to each other than that. But he didn't speak of that. He knew that the pirate chief's mind was set. There was only one more ploy to play.

"And if your ship is lost and sinking, and I am locked in a cage in the hold . . . ?"

"I have a key I have placed on a chain for around your neck that you can wear below your vest. In that eventuality you will have a chance to save yourself."

He had thought of everything. Billy felt defeated and powerless. His body relaxed and he let his arms dangle at his side.

"Yes, I feel my sap rising. I will finish you as master taking captive." The pirate's voice had taken on an excitement and was thick with lust. Billy let his torso arch back, arms dangling, legs trailing beyond the pirate's buttocks, as Khair ad-din came up on his knees in the Octopus position, grabbed Billy's waist and slammed his pelvis down on the pirate's cock. Once, twice, thrice, four . . . . twelve—Billy moaning hard—twenty, twenty-one. And the pirate came in a prodigious gush. He then placed the palm of one hand on Billy's heaving belly to signal that Billy was supposed to remain there, while, with the other, he slowly pumped Billy's cock to ejaculation.

* * * *

It was just as Khair ad-din had predicted. His vessel was far out into the Mediterranean, engaged on three sides by frigates of the U.S. Navy, focusing on the pirate king, determined to lop off the head of the sea dragon.

The pirates had had more than a decade of easy pickings on the sea, especially for the three years that the Americans and

British had been engaged in their own sea war out in the Atlantic and for the years before that that the Americans and French had come close to war. The pirates had resumed taking American ships and demanding ransom for the return of the crews—and Khair ad-din's consortium had been the foremost in this activity. Occupied with troubles closer to home, the United States had been paying the ransom.

The War of 1812 over in early 1815, though, the United States could again turn its sights on the pin-pricking pirates of the Barbary Coast, from Tripoli through Tunisia and Algiers, to Morocco. Shortly after the end of the conflict between the United States and Britain, Tobias Lear, the U.S. consul general in Algiers refused to pay the annual tribute to Algiers and was expelled from the city by the Dey of Algiers, who, as the United States was hoping he would do, declared war on the United States, automatically bringing in Tripoli, Tunis, and Morocco, which were tied to Algiers by mutual defense treaties.

On March 3, 1815, the U.S. Congress authorized a naval force, under heroes of the first Barbary Coast war, Commodores Stephan Decatur and William Bainbridge—Billy's former commander on the *Philadelphia*—to attack the pirates in the Mediterranean. Using the pirate's tactics against them, Decatur and Bainbridge's armada sailed into Algiers harbor, with pirate vessels fleeing the port as the American vessels approached; bombarded the city; and sent Marines in for a land attack. When they pulled back, they took prisoners with them and then, as the pirates had done for centuries, demanded ransom for their return as well as $10,000 for the insult made to the United States. Not much more than a cardboard potentate in real power, the Dey of Algiers capitulated; a treaty was signed on June 30, 1915; and another Barbary Coast war—although not to be the last—was over.

Before attacking Algiers, though, the American fleet moved to thin out the pirates. They did so by targeting Khair ad-din and his motley, if large, fleet of loosely controlled privateers.

Striking at Khair ad-din's vessel at the heart of the consortium, Khair ad-din didn't have a chance when confronted with three U.S. frigates.

The feet that Billy heard on the stairs leading down into the hold of the pirate's flag ship as the battle on deck above was waning were those of American Navy men. They found Billy locked in his cage, dressed in the rags of a merchantman, and well prepared to give his story of thirteen years of captivity on the Barbary Coast. It helped that when William Bainbridge came aboard, he recognized in the thirty-two year old captive the man he had taken on as a naval man at the age of nineteen and who was of the family of wealthy merchantmen.

Billy was steeled to hear that Khair ad-din was dead when he was escorted topside, but he showed no wish to see the body. He just set his face—fighting hard not to show his true feelings—and muttered a "Good. Good riddance," upon being told he was truly free of the man's tyranny.

But Billy knew that it wasn't the U.S. Navy, really, who had set him free. It was his greatest lover, Khair ad-din, who had set him free.

Chapter Ten:

Valletta, Malta, 1815

Billy woke in the late evening and reached over beside him to find the bed empty. He looked over to the French doors out onto the garden on the cliff overlooking Malta's Valetta harbor, with its vast array of ships' masts in view beyond the edge of the garden. He sat up on the side of the bed, opened the drawer of the nightstand, and took out a silver cigarette case, containing rolled cigarettes from Spain, and a box of matches. After lighting up and taking a few puffs, he rose and walked over to the open door and leaned against the frame.

The contrast was interesting. The garden was lush, teeming with tropical flowers and the sounds and sights of the night insects. Crickets were pitching their concerns around the garden, and a frog, in the pond, was responding. Fireflies were making the garden magical. But just beyond that and below the cliff were the masts of an armada of naval vessels, adding a touch of the surreal.

The British navy had made Valletta the base for their Mediterranean fleet the previous year. That's why William Bainbridge had sent Billy here to recuperate, he had told Billy. The Barbary pirates had not remained chastened for long, and this was one of the few safe places in this part of the world where Billy could regain his bearings after more than a dozen years of captivity by what Bainbridge had called "the heathens."

"We cannot risk having you taken by pirates again, William," he had said. "You have suffered enough at their hands."

Bainbridge hadn't asked Billy much about what he had endured in those years, and Billy was reticent about it, willing for Bainbridge to think the worst so that Billy didn't have to tell him Billy's own part in it all. He now, at long last, was able to appreciate why neither Ben nor Khair ad-din had permitted him to become a pirate. He now at least did not have to lie about that and wonder if some victim of the piracy would someday see Billy and accuse him of perpetrating atrocities. The cages had been what kept Billy from constantly having to look over his shoulders now.

"If you don't stop standing there in the moonlight and looking so sexy, I think that I will die of lust," a soft baritone voice spoke from the interior of the garden.

Billy snuffed out his cigarette on the door frame and padded, naked and barefooted, out into the garden.

Wade Burnell was sitting on a stone bench, wrapped in a robe. He too had a Spanish cigarette in his hand, which he flicked off onto the lawn of the garden as Billy approached. Beside him, coming up off his haunches at Billy's approach and fully alert, was the great, black mastiff Wade had told Billy was named Blackie, but which Billy thought of as Son of Freedom.

* * * *

Wade Burnell, a young naval captain, nearly six years Billy's junior, was the U.S. consul general to Malta and the U.S. envoy to the British navy's Mediterranean fleet. Billy had asked about the black mastiff upon his first arrival in Malta, and Burnell had said that, when he was a young lieutenant on his first ship station some four years previously, he had acquired the dog's sire in the capture of a pirate vessel off Algiers. The dog had been despondent except when Burnell had found a bitch for him to breed, and had then died. This was the only male offspring in the resultant litter.

"But a dog on a pirate ship?" Billy had asked, his hands in his pocket so that the consul general couldn't see him trembling. "How did you come to inherit the dog? What of his owners?"

"The dog was the only living thing we took from that privateer ship before we scuttled it," Burnell had answered. "It lived because we could hardly see hanging a dog for piracy. But I don't think we did it a favor. It pined for its lost owner. Dogs have no discernment of the true character of their owners. They are blindly loyal to their master."

Blindly loyal to their master, Billy had thought. He too had pined for Ben for years after Ben had given him away. Was he any better than Freedom in his discernment of the worthiness of his master? And he made no bones about it. Benjamin Palmer had been his master.

Billy had turned away at that, stumbled to a squatting position, and felt like he would vomit. Misinterpreting the problem—thinking that Billy was nearly unhinged from his years as a captive, and believing that a man as small statured, good looking, and well formed as Billy could not have survived without giving the pirates what pirates were well known to want while they were at sea, Burnell had leaned down and gently lifted Billy and slowly helped him to walk into Burnell's bedchamber.

"It need not be as you had it," he had murmured. "I ache for you. If you let me make love to you, I will show you that it can be different from that. I would be good to you."

After having made love to Billy to show him that sex with a man need not always be rough and humiliating, Billy had murmured that the position had been the one of the Elephant, covering the prone Billy closely from above and engaging in that fucking motion that involved only the movement of the two men's pelvises that Billy had come to think of as a camel loping across the dunes of the desert.

Burnell had wondered that Billy had a name for the position, and Billy revealed that he had learned much of the male Kamasutra positions from the Indian eunuchs in the Tripoli palace. The young naval officer, rather than being disgusted or distressed by the refinements of male-on-male sex that Billy had learned, was eager to learn them himself, which led to months of pleasurable training under Billy's instruction.

* * * *

Billy approached Wade in the garden and leaned over and kissed him on the lips. The black mastiff stirred beside Wade, but didn't wake. Wade placed his hands on Billy's naked hips while they were kissing, and when their lips parted he pulled Billy toward him and opened his lips over Billy's cock, making slow love to the phallus. His hands moved around to Billy's buttocks cheeks, which he kneaded while he sucked, pulled apart, and positioned his hands so that he could move an index finger from each hand inside Billy's entrance and tease the hole to open to him.

Billy held Wade's head between his hands and moaned until he felt like he might explode from the attention. Then he gently pulled Wade's mouth off his cock and leaned down and gave him a lingering kiss. While they were kissing, Billy's hands were unknotting the belt at the waist of Wade's robe and opening the thin garment. He reached down and took Wade's cock in both hands.

Wade was already hard for him. Wade was young and virile and in superb shape. This was Billy's first young man who didn't think only of his own pleasure. The Turks and Arabs were satisfying cockers, but lovemaking was not in their lexicon. To those sailors on the *Black Falcon*, Billy had been more of a notch on their leather belts, a rite of passage—marking off having been inside a legendary bottom. And Wade was appreciably younger than he was. Billy had let a young naval lieutenant visit him in his cabin on route to Malta, but he had been close to Billy's age—and had been rough, interested only in getting his rocks off with the small, sexy passenger who had been the subject of rumors of having been the sex slave of Arab pirates for a dozen years and knowing arousing sex techniques from the East. The young lieutenant had left Billy's cabin able to corroborate at least the last of these rumors.

Wade was gentle and sensitive to Billy's needs during a fuck—and he was virile and hard whenever Billy needed him to be hard even if they'd made love several times already in the coupling. He also was eager to learn what Billy had learned about being with a man. All American naval men had heard

144

whisperings about the sex techniques of the East. Billy was teaching them to Wade.

Billy turned and sank his channel on Wade's hard phallus in the sitting position on the bench. As soon as the cock was seated, Billy began to move his pelvis slowly, forward and back.

A groaning Wade, hands gripping Billy's waist, asked, "What again is the name of this position?"

"This is known as the Swing," Billy answered.

"I like this position," Wade murmured between gasps.

"You like all of the positions," Billy said with a small laugh.

"But of course. Can we go through them all tonight? How many are there?"

"More than the night will accommodate. You've heard of the tales of a thousand and one nights, I'm sure. I do believe that the masters of the male Kamasutra have a position to go with each of those nights."

For fifteen minutes they both were lost in the fuck. When Wade had ejaculated, Billy swiveled his torso, careful to hold Wade inside him as he knew this would not be the last of it, and murmured, "Why couldn't you sleep? You've been like this for a couple of days. Is there a worry I can help you with?"

"No one can help me with it, William," Wade answered, using the name that Billy had chosen to use henceforth, now that he was his own man: William Evans Junior. Thirty-two was much too old to be a Billy, even though there were those who would say it still fit his small stature and still miraculously youthful appearance.

"I've been trying to decide how to speak to you of this for days," Wade continued.

"Directly would be good," Billy said, taking Wade's lips with his again. "Whatever needs saying, you can say to me."

"All right then. You have to leave."

"You've grown tired of me?"

"Never," Wade answered. "But I've received dispatches from Washington. I'm sorry to have to tell you, but your father has died, and your mother, who is beyond herself with joy that you are alive, would have you return to take on your father's business and responsibilities."

"Ah, yes, family responsibilities. I have trouble thinking of the needs of anyone other than me. I am not surprised my father has died. It has been many years and he wasn't a well man."

"That's not true that you haven't thought of others; you have taken care of my needs—completely—these last several weeks. It is because of my loss that I've been reluctant to tell you. And there is more."

"More?"

"You have inherited more than your father's business. Another Boston businessman, Benjamin Palmer, has been declared dead too, after a long absence. He was a ship owner and captain as well as a rum and textile manufacturer, and he was thought to have been lost at sea. He has left all he owns to you. You are quite a rich man."

"Ah, gentle Ben. A family friend." It hadn't come as such a blow after weeks of having the chance to adjust to it. He thought of the black mastiff, which often lifted his chin and gave Billy a worshipping gaze, almost as if it realized they had a connection.

"A family friend?" Wade asked.

"One of my earliest lovers."

"Ah, well."

"Knowing that I'm now a rich man, would you be averse to fucking a rich man?" Billy whispered.

"Are you numb inside? Can't you feel me hard inside you again? You will be fucked again now whether you want to be or not."

Billy felt a little of the old thrill of being taken without being consulted. There was a flash of arousal, and he wanted it again—now.

"Have I taught you the Bonobo position yet?" he asked, his voice thick with need. "No matter if I have. That's what I want now. We'll need a firm, yet yielding surface. Your back isn't sore, is it? This will challenge your stamina—but it will be well worth it for both of us. Come, take me inside."

And then, as they struggled to rise from the bench, Billy added, "And, oh, would you be terribly upset if I took Blackie to Boston with me?" If Ben had left him all of his possessions, then the mastiff was really his responsibility too—and his last connection to Ben.

Chapter Eleven:

Boston, 1816

I left the counting house early. Two ships had come in during the morning at Hutchinson's wharf, and the bars on Ship Street should be awash with half-drunk sailors. I went to the Black Falcon Tavern, which I owned, Blackie on a leash trotting beside me. Blackie was always enough to keep me safe. There I sat at my special window overlooking the bar below and ogled the sailors carousing down there—and dreamed of what had been and what I still could have if I was careful—or crazy. I never had been completely cured of the want to be manhandled and punished, and the mere thought of it made me hard. And the boisterous, bald-talking sailors brought up other memories too.

I have frequently over the past year thought of devising some need for business down in Baltimore or up in Providence, somewhere where I would not be recognized. Somewhere that I could find a big-cocked sailor in a dockside bar who I could take to a private room and who would fuck me rough and to memorable exhaustion.

That, however, now seems as much a remote dream as that Ben will walk through the tavern door and Blackie will perk up his ears and turn his head to me and be Freedom again.

Sufficiently hard and aroused, I left the tavern and walked out to the old schoolhouse, no longer on the edge of the city, but enough enclosed by untouched forested lots around it to accord Sam Hale the privacy he seeks from his position at Harvard College. The schoolmaster of my earlier days had bought the schoolhouse and the cottage that went with it when a new schoolhouse was built.

I met him there in his cottage at twilight, and he fucked me in what has become a favorite position for both of us, although I must confess that we are getting more varied in our fucking of late: me on my back with his knees pushed under my buttocks, raising my pelvis to him, and him sliding my channel back and forth on his cock until he has come. Then leaning over me and taking my cock in his mouth and sucking me to ejaculation. We had not gotten to this part when he first fucked me—incompletely—in that position, and I'm fairly sure that in those days I would have come before he did. But I've had much more experience, many more men, and very many more fuckings than he has since our first, failed encounter, and it takes longer to make me come now.

That said, as we become more as one in a melded mechanism of congress, Sam wants me more frequently in each meeting, and in more positions, and he laments that we cannot move against each other, and he in me, through the night. I have visions of him ascending to Mahmud Karamanli's seven-position taking in one session. And I would welcome it from Sam, I think, if I could be with him through the night. It would take me a night to accommodate what Mahmud Karamanli could do with me in an hour. Another reason, I suppose, to dream up imaginary business in Baltimore or Providence.

There are moments when I almost have told him that this favorite position for both of us is the male Kamasutra position of the Octopus. But I've always stopped myself. Somehow I think it more fitting that, between us, we think of it as fucking at the height of our mutual arousal. I cannot stop Sam from discovering that name for it for himself, though. I had learned that from what Sam had told me all those years ago— that it's the equal enjoyment, and the wish that your partner be receiving as much pleasure in the fuck as you are, that is what makes it lovemaking—something very special.

That's why I came back to Sam, why Sam is the only man fucking me now. Because with Sam it is lovemaking and it is equality.

Equality and not being controlled and brutalized is important to me now—despite the edge of lingering desire that sends me to the bars to watch the rowdy sailors and to dream.

As I have written, I probably don't have to tell Sam now that it's the position of the Octopus. He will have read that for himself now, although he never has told me he did.

When we first came back together, no words needing to be spoken. I just walked up to him splitting wood, bare-chested, by the door of the cottage, and he carried me inside to his bed. We were content with just that one fucking, being more interested in hearing what had happened to each of us since our last coupling. But four days later and then just two days after that, and then the very next day, both panting in heat, the Octopus and a sweet encore, usually in the position of the Elephant or the Greyhound—just basic positions to Sam to give him the deepest access and because they set me to moaning more than some of the other positions that require more attention and effort. They are more intimate, I feel. More the positions of lovers.

And the Yin and Yang position. Always, when we feel we want to merge into each other, the Yin and Yang position.

But I ramble. I don't have the facility I should for the storytelling. Sometimes I think it is harder to write about the life than to have lived it.

After our latest encounter, in the dark, I returned home to the house on Foster Lane—to my beautiful bride of six months, Jenny. Twelve years younger than I am, and so deeply infatuated with me that she blushes and casts her eyes down in public but opens her legs and pulls me inside her and begs for the cocking in the privacy of our bedroom. So trusting that she asks little of my past; happy enough that we are so wealthy in the present. And that I have a cock that fills her purse perfectly and as frequently as she asks for it.

After the usual late supper—Jenny assuming that I had been slaving in the nearby offices on Ship Street late—she gave me that look. Even though she is five months gone in her pregnancy, she wanted me inside her. I fucked her gently in what I would tell her was the Spoon position if that didn't lead to more questions and to the unraveling of topics I did not want my choice of having a wife and family to unravel as well. I tried to tell her of the difference between the equality of the slow, gentle fuck and what she says she wanted. But in the end, I took her as she had cried out that she wanted—deep and hard. We climaxed nearly together. She thinks this is magic; she has no idea the training I've acquired to weave this magic.

Jenny says she wants a dozen children. We probably shall—as long as I can continue visiting Sam in his cottage to enjoy true passion. Otherwise I would just as soon withdraw from it all and become as my Indian eunuchs were.

After Jenny drifted off to sleep, I quietly left the bed and climbed the stairs to this room, my old bed chamber, now where I write.

Writing was Sam's idea. He said that I needed to write it all down, both so that I would never forget the events of the last dozen years and so that I could come to grips with it. I didn't want to tell him that I wasn't ashamed by what had happened or traumatized by it, as I was afraid he would think I was an insensitive freak. How can I tell one like Sam that I am addicted to the cock—still? Surely he can understand that by how often I beg for it when we are coupled.

I was rather taken with the idea of writing it down, though. And when I started to, and Sam began reading it, I found—even if he would not admit it—that reading it increased his ardor in our lovemaking.

"The pirate did this to you?" Or, "You moaned when the Arab prince did this with you?" he would murmur upon demonstrating that he had just read of a particular position, and I would answer, "Yes, but not as well as you do." And I would mean it, because he would be doing it to pleasure both of us, not just himself.

We have established a new routine of late, my having found that he is as eager to learn as the consul in Malta was. I take him the chapters as I finish them. He reads them, and then we fuck. Last week, he fucked me for the first time in the position of the Reed before we had even discussed it. That's why

I think he is learning from what he reads—and that he knows which position is that of the Octopus.

When he starts murmuring the names of the positions as we take them up, I suppose I must stop just thinking them myself, and murmur them as well.

He asked me once when we were contemplating a third fucking if the Arab prince fucked me seven times in a session—and the pirate chief twice that, and I put my fingers to his lips and said I was very much younger then and then replaced the fingers with my own lips.

I have no idea what my goal is in writing of these events. No reader would admit reading them; no printer would print them. My early lover, Henry Gawn, very well might, although he very likely would keep the book for himself—and, in any event, he passed while I was in the Mediterranean. I hear that his widow, Marianne, took his last apprentice as a lover and that the town is scandalized by that. I say more power to her—that she should feel free to take her pleasures when, where, and for as long as she is able.

Sam says that someday writings such as these will be read—and even that they will be offered for sale in shops. But I believe that the Harvard College he now teaches at has addled his brain a bit. Thank god his cock still works—very well. He has said I can leave the book in his keeping so that there's no way Jenny will accidentally find it, so as I finish each chapter, I take it to him. And then we fuck. I am content with that.

~

About the Author

Dirk Hessian

An artist and writer, Dirk has always been interested in history and legends, particularly those of the Mediterranean and Asia. His works are historical, and sometimes border on fantasy. They are full of ordinary men struggling to survive and find love in difficult situations. And sometimes Dirk writes about men who are in touch with forces beyond those of mortal men, fighting for survival in more unusual ways.

Dirk's books often, but not always, contain male sex that is both forceful and rough, and at times dangerous, but is always within the context of stories of survival in primitive and brutal times.

You will find Dirk at www.BarbarianSpy.com. Our authors appreciate reviews of their work being posted at distributor and other sites.

FOR LITERARY HEAT

* indicates the book is available in **paperback** and **e-book**.
BOOKS BY CHRIS CROSS
Multisexual Adult Romance
Pulaski Square
Chocolate in Vanilla (MF)
Christmas with Chris (MMF) (MM) (MF)
BOOKS BY ALEX LOCKHEED
Transgender Romance
Meeting Jenna
Transgender Other
Being Sarah
BOOKS BY DIRK HESSIAN

Xtreme Historical Erotica
The King's Men
Shores of Tripoli*
Prophecy of Noto
Pretender's Fate
General Historical Erotic Romance
Puttin on the Ritz
To the Hessian Hills
Fire Down the Valley*
Constantinople*
The Beautiful Way*
Blue and Gray
Colonel's Treasure
Beginning of Time
Labyrinth
BOOKS BY HABU
Gay Erotica
Memoir Faction
Flying High, Diving Deep*
Xtreme Erotica
Liaisons
Chain Gang Banged (Short Story)
Tramp Steaming*
Escape to Girne
Silas' Choice*
Last Call
Choke Hold
Apyko: The Greek Pimp
Visits of the Schlange
Second Coming: Emile La Cour Unleashed*
Vortex: Sacrificed by Curiosity*
Dark Angel Sounding *(in e-book & included in
Sounding:Ultimate Control paperback)**
Sounding: Ultimate Control (*Print Only*)*
Sounding Five *(in e-book & included in
Sounding:Ultimate Control paperback)**
Romance
Finding a New Sam

Bangkok Summer Seduction
The Photograph
Inevitable Case
Turn to Love
Rain Check
Built for Pleasure (Sci Fi)*
Danny's Choice*
Pull of the Groove
Sugar n Spice Christmas
Friday Nights with Lenny (Christmas Romance)
Snowy, Snowy Nights (Christmas Romance)
Tank n Bull
Sail to the Sun
War Letters
Ravens Roost
Caribbean Cruise Top to Bottom
Arena Stage
Trading Partners (Valentine's Day)
Four Coins
Lower Than the Heart (Valentine's Day)
Brambleton
Gotta Keep Trying
Finding Amnad
Platres Conclave
Other Novels/Novellas
Syrian Ram
Temptation's Clutches*
Descent into Chaos
Escape to Girne
Journey Through Abilene
Harmony and Dissonance
Stallion Station
Racing With the Devil (espionage suspense)
Prepared in Cape Verdi
Gilded Cage
House on Park*
Anything for Ambition
Dance of the Ravishers

Hard Knocks U*
My Neighbor's Spa*
Man's Man: Tales of a High Priced Gay Hooker*
Trip Money
The Indian Doctor
Sailorboy
Home to Fire Island
Murder Mysteries
Inevitable Case
Vanishing Laura
Death on a Ping Pong Table
Clint Folsom Mysteries Compendium Volume 1*
Death to Blonds - Stolen Judgment (Clint Folsom
Mystery)*
Clint Folsom Mysteries Compendium Volume 2*
Gay Erotica Anthologies
Earth Cry*
Shunga
Habu's Christmas Balls
Eight in D*
DevilMENt
Silas' Choices*
Stallion Station (A Novella in Parts)
Eleven to the Dogs*
Fifty Seventy*
Spy Tails 001*
Spy Tails 002*
Doubled*
Doubled Again*
Tails in the Tropics*
Tails in the Med*
Tails in the West*
Rough Riders*
Grab Bag 1*
Grab Bag 2*
Grab Bag 3*
Grab Bag 4*
Grab Bag 5*

Grab Bag 6*
Grab Bag 7*
Grab Bag 8*
Grab Bag 9*
Beyond the Beaded Curtain*
Habu's Christmas Balls
The Sporting Life*
Fetish Galore!*
Literary Gay Erotica
Cairo Surrender*
The Handyman*
Homeward Bound
Journey to Mirage*
Bisexual/Menage/Multisexual Erotica
And Eat it Too
Two Men, One Woman*
Every Which Way
Summer of Denial
Death on a Ping Pong Table
Cruising Gigolo
13 Ways for Halloween
Luther*
The Indian Prince*
BOOKS BY SABB
Driver Reliever
Hiring in Hollywood
The Legend of Holleystone Grange
Surprise Encounters*
She is He
Wrong Man
Loyal to his King
Barbarian Tales - Book One - Traveler's Tales*
Barbarian Tales - Book Two - Journeys Begin*
Barbarian Tales - Book Three - The Inheritance*
Barbarian Tales - Book Four - Road to Persepolis*
BOOKS BY SHABBU
Velvet Interrogation
Finding Jason

Dirty Pool
Operation Black Jade
Cigars!*
Angel in the Barn
Gayly Complicated*
Despoiling David
The Tree of Idleness*
I Met a Man
Rough Road to Happiness
BOOKS BY STEPHEN KESSEL
Gay Romance
The Forever Man
Two Chances
BOOKS BY KIM BLACK
Lesbian Romance
Transfixed on Tammie (F/T lesbian)